The Raven League

Buffalo Bill Wanted!

The Raven League:

Buffalo Bill Wanted!

by
Alex Simmons and Bill McCay

SLEUTH
RAZORBILL

The Raven League: Buffalo Bill Wanted!

RAZORBILL/SLEUTH

Published by the Penguin Group
Penguin Young Readers Group
345 Hudson Street, New York, New York 10014, U.S.A.
Penguin Group (USA) Inc., 375 Hudson Street,
New York, New York 10014, U.S.A.
Penguin Group (Canada), 90 Eglinton Avenue East, Suite 700,
Toronto, Ontario, Canada M4P 2Y3 (a division of Pearson Penguin Canada Inc.)
Penguin Books Ltd, 80 Strand, London WC2R 0RL, England
Penguin Ireland, 25 St Stephen's Green, Dublin 2,
Ireland (a division of Penguin Books Ltd)
Penguin Group (Australia), 250 Camberwell Road,
Camberwell, Victoria 3124, Australia
(a division of Pearson Australia Group Pty Ltd)
Penguin Books India Pvt Ltd, 11 Community Centre,
Panchsheel Park, New Delhi – 110 017, India
Penguin Group (NZ), Cnr Airborne and Rosedale Roads,
Albany, Auckland 1310, New Zealand (a division of Pearson New Zealand Ltd)
Penguin Books (South Africa) (Pty) Ltd, 24 Sturdee Avenue, Rosebank,
Johannesburg 2196, South Africa

Penguin Books Ltd, Registered Offices: 80 Strand, London WC2R 0RL, England

10 9 8 7 6 5 4 3 2 1

Use of the Sherlock Holmes characters created by Sir Arthur Conan Doyle
courtesy of the Estate of Dame Jean Conan Doyle.

Library of Congress Cataloging-in-Publication Data is available

Printed in the United States of America

Chapter 1

"CAN YOU MAKE THIS OUT, WIGGINS?" JEAN-BAPTISTE Owens asked.

Archie Wiggins's thin face twisted in concentration as he tried to sound out the first word on the poster. "'B-Buf-Buffalo.'"

The rest was easier. "'Buffalo Bill's Wild West.'"

The bottom of the poster got harder again, but he plowed on. "'America's Na-National Enter-enter—'"

"Entertainment," said Jennie James. "You're getting on well with your reading."

Wiggins shot an annoyed glance at her. "It would come on better if you used a more exciting book to teach us."

"Yeah," said William Doolan, known as Dooley. "All that happens in those stories is that children go to heaven."

"Right," Owens chimed in, pointing at the poster. "Why can't we have stories with cowboys and Indians?"

"We'll be seein' them soon enough," Wiggins said with a grin.

"So you say." Jennie shot a dubious look at the crowd around them. All spring, London and the British Empire had celebrated Queen Victoria's Golden Jubilee. To mark the queen's fifty years on the throne, Londoners had stood at solemn ceremonies and cheered at a grand parade. But they'd also turned out in force to cheer this show that came from America. A good thirty thousand people showed up for each performance of Buffalo Bill's Wild West, paying up to four shillings to get a ticket.

For a boy or girl from the poor East End of the city, even one shilling was a tremendous amount of money. Working every job they could find, Wiggins and his friends had managed to scrape up the train fare to Earl's Court, where the Wild West show appeared as part of the American Exposition. They didn't have enough to pay for tickets, but Wiggins was sure he could get them in somehow. He'd managed to crash the gate at every music hall in the East

End, sometimes in search of clues for the great detective Sherlock Holmes. Most times, however, he'd just wanted a free look at the show.

"Follow me." Wiggins started pushing his way through the crowd. They passed the front of the exhibition building, a huge, shed-like affair that reminded Wiggins of a big train station. The building stretched easily 120 feet, and it extended ten times deeper than that. Its plaster front was already getting a bit grimy, thanks to cinders from passing trains. An American eagle stood over the main entrance, while the Stars and Stripes flapped from a large flagpole. Inside were examples of American know-how—from the way they built steam engines to how their dentists dealt with bad teeth.

Wiggins didn't care about all that, and neither did most of the visitors—except that they had to buy their tickets in the building to get to the outdoor area where Buffalo Bill's Wild West took place. But he knew there had to be entrances where people came in without tickets—performers, workmen, even animals.

A quick glance around showed obstacles, however. The exhibition grounds had started out as wasteland, cut off from the rest of the city by railway lines. These tracks also offered a challenge for would-be gate-crashers. Three railway cuttings created a sort of moat around the Wild West performance area. The only access to the triangular plot of land came from several bridges set across the trenches.

There was a bridge from the exhibition building, but that was for ticket holders. Wiggins settled on a bridge fronting on a roadway as their route in. "Let's try over there," he said.

Jennie nodded toward a figure in blue waving the masses of people past the bridge and toward the ticket offices. "That police constable is sort of in the way."

"There's only one of him," Dooley pointed out.

"All we have to do is wait for our chance," Wiggins said.

A heavy van came rattling up to the bridge. The driver reined in the team of horses, then he jumped off, arranging a set of heavy boards as a ramp. The canvas curtains at the back of the van parted, and a tall, rangy man in a leather vest backed his way down, tugging on a rope.

Londoners dressed in their best—men in straw hats, ladies with parasols, children in sailor outfits—stopped to gawk as the weather-beaten man pulled the rope more sharply.

"He looks like a cowboy," Dooley said.

"Right," Wiggins scoffed. "I'm sure plenty of cowboys work as London—" He broke off when a horned head poked between the canvas panels, something he'd only seen in pictures from Western stories—a buffalo!

The beast stood as large as a horse, maybe bigger, with tightly curled hair covering its humped back and huge head. The rope around its neck like a leash seemed awfully thin.

Another man stepped out beside the buffalo. He also held a lead rope attached to the animal as he carefully stepped past it. This man had high cheekbones, a beak of a nose, and copper-bronze skin.

"I bet he's a Red Indian," Dooley gasped. "A real live savage!"

A final man came out of the van, taking up a station behind the buffalo with a third leash rope. But he didn't look like a Westerner. Wiggins thought he looked like a music-hall comedian. Maybe it was the large, bushy mustache that tried to make up for his sharply receding chin.

Owens nudged Wiggins. "Looks like he left his chin behind in America," he joked.

As the front two men tugged on their ropes, the buffalo came down the ramp to the pavement. Then the creature must have noticed all the people around and stopped dead.

This could be interesting, Wiggins thought. *How do you get a beast that big to move if he doesn't want to?*

The chinless man in the rear tried shoving the buffalo along—without much success.

"He don't know much about animals," Wiggins commented.

The chinless man doubled up the loose end of the rope he held and whacked it across the buffalo's rump. The big beast gave a great jerk, its powerful frame nearly hauling the three handlers off their feet.

Uh-oh, Wiggins thought. If an animal that size spooked and tried to run through the crowd, people were going to get hurt. He grabbed Dooley's shoulder and began backing them away. From the corner of his eye, he saw Jennie retreating with Owens. Those around them shifted about, uncertain whether to continue watching or move away.

The buffalo gave a great snort, twisting around as if looking for a way to escape. The police constable, obviously realizing the danger, pushed forward. "All right, now," he told the onlookers. "Move along and let the men do their work."

The Indian dropped his rope and turned to push through the tightly clustered knot of spectators.

"Silent Eagle," the cowboy in the leather vest called. "Where are you going?"

The Indian gave no reply, disappearing into the crowd. Wiggins saw Jennie on tiptoe, trying to see where the Indian went. She looked nervous. No wonder—two men couldn't control such a big animal alone.

The chinless man raised his rope as if to whip the buffalo again.

"You blasted fool!" yelled the weather-beaten cowboy—too late. The gesture was enough to spook the animal. With a bellow, the buffalo began trying to shake loose from the ropes around its neck. The creature's heavy shoulder hit the cowboy hard enough to send him stumbling.

Perhaps that Indian had the right idea, running off, Wiggins thought as scared crowd members jostled him, struggling back from the buffalo.

The police constable's face went pale, but he stepped in front of the beast.

"What's he going to do?" Jennie gasped.

Wiggins wasn't sure. A blow from the constable's truncheon wouldn't even faze the buffalo, and the man certainly couldn't hope to wrestle with the big brute.

"He's trying to get its attention," Wiggins realized. "If it charges, it'll come for *him*." Wiggins had to give the copper grudging respect for bravery. It might be the only way to protect the people crowded around, but it would probably kill the man.

Suddenly someone shoved past Wiggins, heading straight for the snorting, stomping beast. It was the Indian! He held his hands cupped together, opening them up as he came to the buffalo.

The enormous animal thrust his nose at the Indian's hands. A huge, pinkish tongue came out to swipe up some of the grain the man held out.

The police constable laughed. "Clever! You went and got the beastie some food. And here I thought you'd run off like a yellow dog." He winked. "Or rather, a *red* dog!"

His comment brought an angry look from the Indian, who backed away, still holding out the grain. The buffalo followed him, almost dragging the other two handlers along with him, while the constable and the crowd looked on and laughed.

Now, Wiggins decided. *While they're all watching the buffalo.* "Come on," he whispered. He jerked his head toward the bridge.

As they dashed across the bridge, Wiggins heard the policeman still joking with the Indian. "With you folk, I figured you'd rather eat 'im instead of feeding him."

"He don't have to keep mockin' him," Owens said.

"Who?" Dooley asked.

"That copper keeps poking fun at the Indian."

"He didn't really say anything that bad," Jennie commented.

Owens glanced from the constable to his friends, frowning but saying nothing.

They were across now, past the tall fences that blocked the view from the street. Another fence stretched off to their right. Judging from the sounds coming from beyond it, Wiggins figured that was the corral where cattle and buffalo roamed. Straight ahead, an enormous mound of dirt and rocks rose in three irregular peaks, the largest about thirty feet high. Wiggins couldn't imagine what it was doing there. Maybe it had been left over after workmen leveled the area for the Wild West show.

Curving away from the artificial hill were large canvas walls mounted on wooden frames. "What are those?" Jennie asked.

"It's the back of painted scenery," Wiggins said. "I seen it in theaters, but these things are enormous!"

"Won't give us anyplace to blend in and disappear," Owens pointed out. Through openings in the canvas, they could see the vast open space of an arena with grandstands of seats in the distance.

"So where do we go?" Dooley asked nervously.

"I'm not sure," Wiggins admitted. Wiggins's eyes went wide as he shifted from looking for a hiding place to actually taking in what was before him.

People in colorful costumes were brushing horses or mounting them.

"Wow," Wiggins exclaimed. "These must be the folk who put on the show!"

"Who are those fancy lads?" Owens pointed toward dark-skinned men in silk and embroidered velvet. "I saw them on the posters."

"They're Mexicans," Jennie replied. "I read about them in the newspapers."

"I'm sure you did, Little Miss Bookworm," Wiggins muttered under his breath. Jennie's schoolmarm airs still irritated him—even though her ability to read had helped them solve their first case.

Wiggins shook off the feeling, focusing on their surroundings. He saw cowboys in really fancy clothes. They wore broad-brimmed hats with brightly colored sashes around their middles. Cowgirls in brightly colored jackets and hats swung up onto gleaming saddles. Then there were the Indians, showing much bronzed skin in tattoos and paint, with large, feathered warbonnets.

"Step lively," Wiggins hissed. "Look like you know where you're going. And don't gawk, Dooley!"

They set off. As Wiggins had hoped, the various

riders were more absorbed in their own preparations than in any passing children. Wiggins had just seen what a spooked animal could do, so he avoided walking under any horse's nose.

"Hoy! What are you brats doing here?" a voice behind them blared out.

Wiggins glanced over his shoulder to see the man Dooley had called a cowboy. From the look on the fellow's lined, tan face, they could count themselves lucky that he didn't have one of those six-shooter revolvers. Wiggins broke into a run, pulling his friends along.

If we get up on the artificial hill, he thought, *maybe it will be too much trouble for him to come up after us.*

It was their only hope. "Climb!" Wiggins ordered.

He leaped atop a jutting rock and began scrambling higher. Jennie was right behind him. *The show must be starting soon. If we can get high enough and hide, this gink will have other jobs to do. He'll have to give up.*

Wiggins's hopes were dashed when he heard a cry from below. He looked down to see that the man had managed to grab one of Dooley's ankles. The boy clung to a scraggly bush above him, but it was obvious he couldn't maintain that hold very long.

"Got you," the man said in grim satisfaction. "The rest of you had better get down here, or I'll snap his leg like a twig."

Wiggins, Jennie, and Owens made their unwilling way downward even as Dooley tried to wriggle free.

"Zeke!" A voice rang out from ground level. Dooley's captor almost lost his grip on the boy when he glanced back over his shoulder. A figure in gleaming white buckskin with a long decorative fringe stepped up to the hill.

Wiggins stared as the man came closer, taking in his long auburn hair, his neat imperial chin whiskers and mustache, the broad-brimmed Stetson hat he wore. It was the same face he'd seen pictured on the posters for the Wild West show.

The legendary Buffalo Bill Cody himself!

Chapter 2

"I DON'T SEE ANY NEED TO FRIGHTEN KIDS, ZEKE." Cody's voice was calm, yet commanding. "Do you?"

The roustabout glanced from his prisoner to Cody's steely gaze. "Guess not," he mumbled, releasing Dooley. Without giving the children a second look, Zeke turned and walked away.

Cody smiled. "I expect you should run on back to your folks."

Wiggins started to reply, but Dooley spoke first. "Oh, we didn't come with our folks," he announced. "My da is working the docks, and me mum is dead."

"Sorry to hear that," Cody replied. "But who—"

He didn't get a chance to finish as Dooley slid back to the ground and thrust out his hand. "I'm Dooley, and this here is Wiggins, Owens, and Jennie." Dooley glanced sheepishly at the colonel. "I should have introduced her first 'cause she's a girl. But she's all right."

"Well, thanks," Jennie muttered.

"Glad to meet you all," Cody told them. "I take it you got in here a little bit less than the proper way."

Wiggins stepped in. "We weren't trying to rob nobody or do any mischief," he explained. "It's just we . . . we . . ."

"We've never seen anything like this, ever," Jennie finished.

"And it took everything we earned for days just to get here," Dooley said.

Cody frowned. "Are all of you without parents?"

"No," Owens replied. "Jennie, Wiggins, and me have mothers. But it's all they can manage to make ends meet. They don't have time to be seeing shows and such."

"We should be working too," Wiggins said. "But all London is talking about your show, and we just had to see it."

Cody smiled. "Well, then, you should be getting a look."

Wiggins could barely contain his excitement as Buffalo Bill gave him and his friends a tour. They strolled among the bustling performers, then along twisting paths weaving among a confusing array of tents. Colonel Cody pointed to a man carefully checking the saddle on his horse. "That's Marve Beardsley. He shows how the Pony Express riders used to change horses and switch mailbags on the run, just as he did back when." Cody glanced over at Wiggins. "That was one of *my* first jobs. I wasn't much older than you."

"I wish I could have adventures like that." Wiggins sighed.

"You do!" Owens said. He turned to Buffalo Bill. "Wiggins works for Sherlock Holmes."

Cody looked surprised. "The famous detective?"

"In fact, we all do—sometimes," Jennie said.

"Yeah, the four of us helped him with a big case." Dooley nearly stumbled over a tent rope, he was so distracted talking to Buffalo Bill.

The tour ended at a large white canvas tent near one end of the grandstand. "This one's mine," Cody said.

A canvas partition created two rooms. The main area contained some folding chairs, a desk filled with papers, and kerosene lamps with frosted glass globes.

Dark green fabric above them kept things cool and shady, and animal hides lay spread across the ground as rugs.

Wiggins got a glimpse of a washstand, a clothing rack filled with costumes, and the corner of a cot in the other room.

He turned to see Owens poke a careful toe at the clawed paw still attached to a grizzly bear hide. Jennie stared at the animal's head and teeth.

"Now," Cody said as he motioned his guests to sit down. "I have to go on in a few minutes, so why don't you all make yourselves comfortable while I get ready?" He went into the second room. Wiggins heard water pouring into a basin.

"How come you're being so nice to us?" Dooley asked.

Cody came back out, mopping his face with a towel. "I had a son of my own." He glanced at Dooley. "He was a bit younger than you—" He suddenly broke off.

"Oh," Jennie said in a small voice.

"I was away doing a show when he got sick." Cody's eyes became haunted. "By the time I got home, he was almost gone. I held him all night, but I couldn't keep him with us."

Dooley ran to Colonel Cody and took his hand. "I lost someone too. It was bad—very bad."

"Your mother?" Cody asked gently.

"That was when I was real young. But we lost my brother, Tim, a couple of months ago. He and Wiggins both worked for Mr. Holmes. They followed some suspicious folks and got trapped in an opium den. Tim—didn't make it out."

Cody glanced at Wiggins with new respect. "Did Mr. Holmes catch the killer?"

"*We* did," Dooley replied proudly. "We worked with Mr. Holmes."

Cody's eyes were still on Wiggins, who bit his lip. "It doesn't change things," he said in a low voice. "Tim's still . . ."

Cody stepped over to put a hand on Wiggins's shoulder. "Son, you didn't set out to put him in harm's way."

"No, but he wouldn't have been there if it weren't for me," Wiggins told the frontiersman.

"So you blame yourself." Cody nodded. "Does Dooley blame you?"

"I did at first," Dooley admitted. "That was before we all joined together in the Raven League, caught the killer, and rescued Mr. Holmes. We even—"

"Dooley!" Owens said sharply. "You know better."

Cody glanced at the foursome. "Something wrong?"

"We're not supposed to talk about it," Wiggins explained. "Sorry."

"Let's just say," Jennie offered, "that Mr. Holmes was able to catch the criminals he was after."

"Thanks to us—the Raven League," Dooley put in.

Wiggins couldn't tell if the frontiersman believed them or not. Before anyone could say any more, a short, dark-haired man with a carefully trimmed full beard appeared in front of the tent.

"Colonel, you're on in three minutes!"

"Sorry, Nate," Cody apologized, "I got caught up jawing with my visitors. Kids, this is Nate Salsbury. He's my partner in the show."

The children all greeted the man, who gave them a distracted nod while still looking at Cody. "Get your coat on and let's go! Don't you wear your six-gun?"

Colonel Cody glanced at the gun belt hanging from a hook on one of the tent poles. "Here it—" He stopped. The holster was empty. "Now, where the devil is that Colt?"

Nate joined him in a quick search, but the pistol wasn't anywhere in the tent.

"A six-gun!" Jenny said. "That sounds dangerous."

Cody shook his head. "It's only loaded with blanks. Still . . ." He frowned.

"Maybe one of the boys took it for a cleaning," Nate suggested. "You said the action was a little sluggish."

"Maybe," Cody said cautiously. "But I'd think they would have said something."

Salsbury glanced at his watch. "You're supposed to be mounted up by now. Just grab a gun on the way."

An Indian brave walked into the tent. He wore leggings with brightly embroidered borders, a long blue shirt that almost reached his knees, and a rawhide vest decorated with quills and purple beads. A colorful painted design covered his face, and he wore a feathered headdress. Wiggins almost didn't recognize him, but the man's dark, brooding eyes were unmistakable. "That's the same Indian who stopped the buffalo from running wild," he whispered to his friends.

"I've come to get Pahaska," the Indian explained. "The riders are waiting."

"We know that, Silent Eagle," Nate replied with annoyance. "Who made you stage manager?"

The Indian's eyes narrowed, but he didn't respond.

"Now, boys," Colonel Cody said as he slipped on his gun belt. "There's no time for this. We've got a show to do." He pointed at the pistol tucked in Silent Eagle's belt. "Can I borrow that?"

Without a word, Silent Eagle passed over the gun, turned, and walked out of the tent.

"What about them?" Nate glanced at the kids.

"Why, these members of the Raven League are my guests," Cody informed him. "You find them someplace to watch the show while I go mount up."

Nate Salsbury led Wiggins, Owens, Jennie, and Dooley up a narrow aisle at the far side of the grandstand. This was a huge roofed structure forming a crescent halfway around the performance arena.

Staring around at the standing-room-only crowd, Wiggins wondered if half of London had come to see the show. He turned to the arena, which reminded him of a racetrack—a large dirt oval with grass in the center. Beyond rose the other side of the artificial hill with additional landscaping—trees and bushes—flanked by painted scenery showing Western mountains and a big sky.

A man climbed onto a rostrum at the side of the track. "LADIES AND GENTLEMEN!" The man must have had lungs of leather to be heard over the crowd noise, even with a megaphone in his hand. "Buffalo Bill and Nate Salsbury proudly present America's National Entertainment, the one and only, genuine and authentic, unique and original . . . Wild West!"

The audience cheered politely at first, then with more enthusiasm as Indians, Mexican riders, and American cowboys rode past in a grand procession. Colonel Cody came riding out on a large white stallion. The performers wheeled into a line, suddenly surging toward the grandstand at a full gallop.

Hundreds of hooves pounded the earth. War whoops and yells filled the air—and in the lead rode Buffalo Bill!

Wiggins held his breath as the stampede rumbled right for him. At the last possible second, the colorful line of riders came to a perfect halt, kicking up clouds of dust. Wiggins and everyone else went wild. Dooley couldn't contain himself, leaping about as he cheered.

For the next hour, Wiggins found himself transported to a different world of wild sights and rugged pastimes. He and his friends chattered excitedly as they saw exhibitions of trick shooting, roping, and riding.

Other times, Wiggins completely forgot anyone was with him as he became lost in dramatic scenes. Indians attacked a wagon train, a stagecoach full of special guests, and a settler's cabin—but every time, Buffalo Bill Cody and the cowboys came riding to the rescue.

The Indians showed off their special skills, riding races against one another, demonstrating a war dance. They also showed grimmer talents, seizing captives by the hair, slashing with a glittering knife, and holding up a reddened scalp!

Shocked, Wiggins glanced at the other members of the Raven League. Jennie turned away while Dooley hid his eyes. "That wasn't real!" Owens insisted in a hoarse voice.

It wasn't—the prisoners soon reappeared in other scenes, safe and sound, though Wiggins found it hard to keep track of them as the arena swirled with wild scenes, thundering hooves, echoing gunshots, and deafening applause. By the time the show ended, Wiggins's hands hurt as he and his friends filed out with the crowd.

The members of the Raven League faced a long walk back to Mile End Road in London's East End. But reliving the amazing action they'd seen made the trek seem easier.

"We've got to come back tomorrow!" Owens enthusiastically cried.

"How?" Jennie raised the practical question. "We've no money left at all. And we were lucky today, sneaking in as we did. If Colonel Cody hadn't come along, that fellow would have tossed us out on our backsides."

Wiggins laughed, but he had to agree with her. It would take a while to raise some money to come back—train fare, at least. For the rest, well, they'd snuck in once. Could they do it again?

"You have to admit," he said to Jennie, "that was a bit of all right, wasn't it?"

"A bit?" Jennie's face beamed. "It was the most wonderful thing I've ever seen. I plan to write everything down so I'll remember." She held up her special treasure, the little notebook and pencil Dr. Watson had given her. Her smile dimmed a bit. "But I won't be writing about how the Indians took that man's hair off. Scalping, they called it."

"Not just them," Wiggins told her. "Even Buffalo Bill lifted a scalp back when he was fighting the Indians, or so I hear."

"My mother's cousin wrote a story about that when the Wild West show first came to London," Owens said.

The others nodded. They knew Owens's relative worked for a small West Indian newspaper in the city.

"It was after the Indians had wiped out a detachment of cavalry," Owens began.

"Custer's Last Stand," Dooley eagerly put in.

Owens nodded. "I wouldn't want those savages coming after me. A bad lot, they are."

"Those red devils wouldn't last long in London," Dooley insisted.

"They're brave, though," Jennie said. "We saw how dangerous one buffalo could be. Imagine riding into a herd of them—hundreds. That's what Indians do when they hunt the creatures."

"Well." Wiggins chuckled. "If they're such a wonder to you, maybe we'll let 'em scalp *you* tomorrow."

The others laughed—even Jennie, after clouting the boys once or twice each.

They finally reached the crowded tenements of London's poorest section. Despite the grim surroundings, the day's colorful events filled Wiggins's mind as he went home.

The visions stayed with him when he woke up the next morning. After a quick breakfast—a stale bread roll dunked in sweet tea—Wiggins set off on errands for some local merchants. Jennie was right. A day off had been a grand thing, but now each of them had to earn money.

At the end of the day he was hot and tired as he trudged along Whitechapel Road, heading back to his neighborhood. Should he see if his friends were about or just go home and rest? As he came to Mile End Road, he heard a newsboy calling out the headline of the day. Wiggins suddenly froze, listening.

"Extree! Extree!" the lad shouted. "Savage attack in Earl's Court! Horrible crime at American Exhibition! Constable attacked . . . shot and scalped! Shot and scalped!"

Chapter 3

DIGGING IN HIS POCKET, WIGGINS CAME UP WITH A penny to buy the newspaper. One look at the crowded columns of type and he shook his head, grumbling. "I can't read this." Folding up the paper, he headed for the Raven Pub.

Mr. Pilbeam, the pub owner, allowed Wiggins, Owens, Jenny, and Dooley to use the Raven's back room as a clubhouse of sorts. Faced with deadly peril while trying to solve the mysterious disappearance of Sherlock Holmes, Wiggins and his friends had pledged to help one another, forming the Raven League. Some people thought the name came from the ravens that lived at the Tower of London. Legend had it that if these birds ever left, the British Empire would fall. In truth, though, the group named itself after the place where the four had made their pact.

He was in luck. Everyone had stopped by today.

"Have you heard what the newsboys have been crying up?" Wiggins waved the newspaper.

"I was hoping they were saying things that weren't actually in the story," Jennie replied.

"Read it, then," Wiggins said, holding out the paper. "It's too much for me."

Jennie frowned as she scanned the page. "'Shocking attack at Earl's Court,'" she read the first headline. "'Police constable near death. Barbaric act of cruelty.'" Her face grew grimmer as she read on.

"Well?" Owens pressed. "We're waiting."

"Do they talk about Indians?" Dooley asked.

"It says an off-duty police constable was shot at the Earl's Court exhibition grounds."

"Plenty of posh folk around there," Wiggins said. "That would draw the local villains."

Jennie shook her head. "The policeman was found in the stables of the Wild West show."

"What was the copper doing there?" Owens asked.

"No one knows," Jennie replied. "He was unconscious when he was found." She hesitated, then read from the paper. "'A heavily engraved revolver was found near the stricken policeman. It was identified as a weapon that had been presented to Colonel William F. Cody, an American more commonly known as Buffalo Bill.'"

"They're trying to make it out that Buffalo Bill did it?" Owens said in surprise.

"There's more." From Jennie's expression, Wiggins knew it wasn't good. "While the constable lay helpless, he was . . . abused."

"Abused?" Wiggins echoed. "How?"

"His attacker used a knife to remove the constable's hair—his scalp."

Dooley's eyes went big. "He was scalped? Maybe there was an Indian involved. Who else would do something like that?"

Jennie looked troubled. "When we were coming home from the show, Owens mentioned Buffalo Bill scalping someone," she said.

"That was during a war!" Dooley exclaimed. "After Custer's Last Stand."

"It happened during the last great wars with the Indians," Owens said. "Buffalo Bill was serving as a scout with another part of the army, trying to keep more tribes from joining the uprising."

He screwed up his face, trying to remember all the details. "Buffalo Bill and the leader of the war party fought each other. The Indian's shot missed. Buffalo Bill's didn't. Then he noticed that the dead Indian was wearing a long blond scalp that had come from a woman. Cody got so angry, he scalped the chief, holding it up to the troopers riding past and shouting, 'First scalp for Custer!'"

Wiggins let out a long breath. "I'd heard some of that, but not all of it."

Dooley leaned forward, all excited. "I saw a picture of it in a magazine once." He frowned. "But I didn't know what it was about, and it didn't show any blood."

Wiggins gave him a look. "They wouldn't, in a proper magazine." He glanced at Jennie. "It ain't respectable."

She folded the paper. "Respectable or not, maybe other people have seen that picture. Or someone might reprint the story, especially since Colonel Cody's gun was found beside the policeman. What do you imagine those people will think?"

Dooley's face went nearly as red as his hair. "Buffalo Bill wouldn't do nothing like what you said!" Wiggins could see the hero worship in the boy's eyes as he spoke.

"I don't think so either," Wiggins said slowly, but doubt crept into his voice. Working for Sherlock Holmes, he had learned that people could do all sorts of things—especially rich, famous people.

"You don't sound so sure," Owens challenged. It was clear that Colonel Cody had impressed him too.

Wiggins shrugged.

"Why would Buffalo Bill lift the scalp from a copper, of all people?" Owens pressed.

"I'm not saying he did," Wiggins replied. "It's just that I remember something Mr. Holmes told Dr. Watson. He said, 'Only the clues should lead one to the culprit—nothing else.' What that means is, none of us should assume Buffalo Bill is guilty *or* innocent. We should look at the clues."

"I don't know if the scalping was a clue," Jennie said. "But the newspaper made a big thing about the gun found beside the policeman belonging to Colonel Cody."

"I don't care if they found him standing over the copper with a bloody knife," Dooley said hotly. "Buffalo Bill helped us and was nice to us. I'll tell anyone—"

"Wait a tick," Wiggins interrupted. "The gun

belonged to Buffalo Bill. That doesn't mean he used it. He didn't even have it when he was supposed to go on for the show. Remember?"

"You're right!" Owens said excitedly. Dooley nodded vigorously.

Even Jennie had to agree. "That could be a clue," she said. "Shouldn't we make sure the police know it as well?"

It was a long walk from Mile End Road in the East End to Charing Cross in the middle of London. With every step, a little more of Wiggins's confidence leaked away. The police didn't like the poor folk of the East End, and the feeling was mutual. Out in the street, Wiggins and his mates had made some coppers' lives difficult. And by working for Sherlock Holmes, he'd often helped to make the police look foolish. They couldn't expect a warm welcome at Scotland Yard.

When they turned off onto Whitehall, Wiggins saw a policeman he knew, but the man wasn't in uniform. Inspector Desmond wore a well-cut suit, standing out from the shabbier figures cut by some detectives. Wiggins had seen him around the

East End, guiding posh folk wanting a look at the "lower classes."

The policeman was also a well-known figure to London newspaper readers. Not surprising, Wiggins thought. Outgoing, with ruddy good looks and a carefully clipped reddish brown mustache, Desmond charmed most of the city's reporters. Now, though, he didn't look charming. He seemed downright angry as a short, portly man chewed his ear.

Wiggins's eyes went wide as he recognized the second man—J. Montague Pryke. Like most East Enders, Wiggins, Dooley, and Owens knew him by sight.

"Who is that?" Jennie asked.

"That's Mr. Pryke," Wiggins replied. "He's an MP, a Member of Parliament. He represents the East End in the House of Commons."

"He's a fiery one," Owens chimed in. "He gets people all stirred up with his speeches. Always saying he's one of us and all."

Wiggins puffed up his chest and tucked his thumbs behind his jacket lapels. "I come from humble beginnings," he said, trying to sound like a politician.

The kids chuckled as they glanced over at the man. Pryke's pudgy face wasn't humble as he glared at Inspector Desmond, even if he had to look up at the policeman. The MP's extravagantly curled mustache seemed to bristle as he loudly complained.

"The people of London, not to mention your fellow officers, expect a quick resolution to this barbaric attack on one of our own policemen," Pryke barked. "We also expect that you, as the head of the investigation, will be firm with these uncivilized American visitors. Scotland Yard has shown itself to be remarkably lax when dealing with, shall we say, a certain—*class* of criminal."

Pryke's voice grew louder and his words echoed off the arched stone ceiling above. "A common burglar could expect to spend the next few years in Dartmoor after being captured. But what happens to a society jewel thief like 'Gentleman' Jeremy Clive? Just because he went to the right schools and has the right friends, he somehow manages to escape from his cell. Now you and your superiors are coddling this collection of Yankee cutthroats and out-and-out savages. Like yourself, this Buffalo Bill person is very popular in the higher social circles. Has the Yard become timid in the face of a celebrity? Or could it be——"

Pryke gave Desmond a long, slow wink. "Did the word to go slowly come from the 'higher-ups'?"

"What does he mean by that?" Dooley asked.

Wiggins motioned for Dooley to be silent. There was tension in the air, and he half expected the Scotland Yard man to explode with anger at this insulting hint. Instead, Desmond took a deep breath but ignored the remark. "The constable is in the hospital, and we've been unable to get any statement. If you'll excuse me, I'm off to Bart's to see him right now." He tipped his bowler hat and set off down the passageway.

Wiggins darted after the policeman. "Inspector——"

Desmond barely glanced back. "I've no need of anything a street Arab may be selling," he said gruffly.

"Street Arabs" was what respectable Londoners called the children who roamed the streets looking for any kind of work to earn a few pennies.

Wiggins had heard solid citizens talk about these street kids as if they were barely a jump above the savages Buffalo Bill had brought to town.

Owens spat on the pavement in disgust. "Don't even bother. He ain't interested in hearing from the likes of us."

"Maybe we should take this to Mr. Holmes," Jennie suggested. "He'd certainly listen to us."

"And the coppers'll listen to him," Dooley added.

"No," Wiggins replied. "Not yet. I've got a better idea!"

Chapter 4

WIGGINS STARTED EASTWARD BACK ALONG THE STRAND.
"We've got to get to St. Bartholomew's Hospital!"

"Why?" Dooley asked in surprise. "You sick?"

Wiggins rolled his eyes. "No. Inspector Desmond said he's going to Bart's to see the injured copper, so that's where we need to be."

"Are you daft?" Owens exclaimed. "They're not going to let us in to see him, no matter how nice we ask."

"Good," Wiggins said with a smile. "Because we're not going to ask. We're going there to see what we can see, hear what we can hear. Desmond said the copper hasn't talked yet. I want to know what he says when he does."

"Why?" Jennie asked.

Wiggins was already moving down the street. "We know someone took Colonel Cody's gun yesterday," he replied, "and it looks like they used it on the constable——"

"So they can frame Buffalo Bill!" Owens finished as he caught up with Wiggins, Jennie and Dooley close behind. "But who, and why?"

"Maybe they were stealing the gun and the constable caught them," Dooley suggested.

"I don't think so," Jennie said. "The gun went missing hours before the officer was attacked."

"Well, let's go and find out!" Wiggins led the others at a half run to Fleet Street, turning left onto the Old Bailey. The hospital rose before them, its gray stone walls grimy with more than a hundred years of soot, but still large and majestic.

Wiggins and the others stood watching for some way to enter without being stopped. "One or two of us might slip in," Wiggins told them. "But not all four of us."

Suddenly he spotted a distressed woman hurrying toward the hospital gate. She had three children scurrying along behind her and a small baby in her arms.

"Right!" Wiggins cried. "Jennie, Dooley, tag after that lot. Look like you belong with them till you get inside."

"Then what?" Dooley asked.

"We look for the inspector," Jennie replied, grabbing Dooley's hand, "or the injured copper. Come along!"

Wiggins grinned as Jennie hurried with Dooley across the street. He was pleased at how quickly she'd picked up on his idea.

Guess she's starting to fit in! Wiggins thought as he leaned against a lamppost.

"What'll we do now?" Owens asked as they watched their friends trail the family into the hospital.

Wiggins replied with a shrug. "We wait."

"Where's the casualty ward?" the upset woman called as she came through the arched gateway. As she was being directed to a building on the left, Jennie and Dooley took advantage of the brief hesitation to join the family. Only one of the children seemed to notice them as they trailed along to another building—the others were too focused on their mother.

Coming in the entrance, the frantic woman clutched at the arm of a short woman in a white bonnet and apron. "My husband was hurt across the way in the meat market. They told me he was brought here."

"Here" was a large, dim, echoing room, full of sick people and medical staff moving among them.

"What is his name?" the nurse asked.

Jennie didn't hear the reply over the noise of coughing, babies crying, clanking instruments, and walking feet. She guided Dooley off to the side of the crowded scene.

"Where are we going?" Dooley asked.

"Take a look." She nodded to their right, where Inspector Desmond stood talking to a tired-looking man in a rumpled suit—a doctor, she imagined. Close by the two men stood some sort of cart piled high with sheets and towels.

Jennie realized that if she and Dooley could get behind the cart, they could overhear without being seen. "Follow me," she whispered to Dooley.

Jennie and Dooley waited until a nurse came out from behind a framed screen, carrying away a bundle of bloody linens in her arms. Then they scuttled for the cart.

They must keep the most sick or injured people beyond there, Jennie thought.

She and Dooley were close enough now to hear the inspector's voice even with the racket around them.

"It's vitally important that I speak to him, Doctor," Desmond said.

"I understand that," the doctor replied. "But Constable Turnbuckle has received grievous injuries—powder burns on his face, though we found no wound. Then he was beaten severely."

"I know that, but—"

"It is a miracle that he is still alive," the doctor added. "He lost a great deal of blood from the scalping."

"And the longer I wait to speak to him, the farther away his attacker can fly."

"Very well, Inspector." The doctor threw up his hands. "But be aware he is hardly in his right mind."

"Yes, yes," Desmond replied. "I'll be on my best behavior." Inspector Desmond and the doctor stepped behind the screen.

Jennie peeked from around the cart. She could see the foot of a bed and part of the inspector's back as he bent forward. A gas jet on the wall gave slightly better light. Creeping up to the screen itself, she got a glimpse of the patient. Constable Turnbuckle lay on his back, still and quiet. His head was wrapped in white bandages, but Jennie could see small brown stains on the top and sides.

"Speak softly, Inspector," the doctor cautioned. "I don't want him upset in any way."

Jennie could see the inspector's lips move, but she couldn't hear what he was saying over the noise in the rest of the great hall. The injured officer's moans and mumblings were even less intelligible.

"I've got to get closer," she whispered to Dooley.

Dooley pulled her away from the partition. "You planning to turn invisible?" he demanded. "That inspector will see you and toss us both out."

Jennie looked around, spotting a pail of dingy gray water and an old mop. She grabbed two towels from the cart, tying one around her waist like an apron. The other she wrapped about her head, covering her hair. With trembling hands, she wrung out the mop and began slowly swabbing her way around the screen.

"Be ready to run if this doesn't work," she whispered to Dooley, who remained hidden behind the cart.

Inspector Desmond and the doctor had their backs to her as she moved closer, still pretending to mop the floor.

"Constable Turnbuckle," the inspector said softly, as if trying to wake a sleeping child. "I repeat. Did you see who assaulted you?"

Now Jennie could hear the constable's replies, though that didn't make them easier to understand.

"Smug . . . ga . . . saw him . . ."

"Who did you see?" the inspector asked.

"Inspector, please," the doctor warned.

"Just another moment." The inspector leaned in closer. "Did someone shoot you?"

"Buffalo . . . stop . . . smug . . . smuggling."

The inspector quickly turned toward the doctor. "Did you hear that? You're a witness."

"Yes," the doctor replied cautiously. "But to what?"

The inspector looked just as puzzled as the doctor. "I'm not sure, Doctor. At least, not yet."

Jennie felt she had pressed her luck as far as it would go. She had not been noticed, but it was only a matter of time before the two men saw her or someone else came in. She slipped back around the screen.

Dooley jumped out of hiding. "What did you hear?"

"Let's get out first," Jennie hissed. She discarded her disguise by the cart and hustled Dooley out of the building.

They rushed across Giltspur Street to where Wiggins and Owens leaned against a lamppost. Both boys came alert.

"What happened?" Wiggins asked.

"The constable is hurt badly." Jennie shuddered at the memory of the bloody bandages. "But he mumbled a few things."

Jennie quickly repeated what she had heard in the hospital room.

"Well, what is that supposed to mean?" Owens asked.

"The inspector had no idea either," Jennie replied.

Wiggins ran a hand through his bristly hair. "Sounds like he's talking about smuggling something. But what?"

"He also said 'buffalo,'" Jennie reminded them. "Do you think he meant that Buffalo Bill is a smuggler?"

"He wouldn't do that!" Dooley burst out angrily. "He's a hero, and he wouldn't shoot a policeman either."

Wiggins's stomach tensed as he searched for something to say. He liked Buffalo Bill too, but he'd also heard Sherlock Holmes say so many times, "Never let emotions affect your thinking on a case." To Wiggins, this meant that a villain could be just as likable as a hero—Colonel Cody could be guilty somehow.

He was about to share his thoughts with the others when he spotted Inspector Desmond exiting the hospital.

"Let's try to tell him about the missing gun again," Wiggins said. "He might listen this time."

This time the inspector did stop, but after listening to their story, he shook his head. "I already know about that gun."

"But how?" Wiggins asked.

"Oh, one of Colonel Cody's people told me," Desmond replied. "But it doesn't really matter, as—"

"What do you mean?" Dooley exploded. "It's very important! It proves Colonel Cody couldn't have used it against that copper."

Desmond slowly turned toward Dooley, his dark brown eyes boring into the boy's. "Actually," he said calmly, "it proves nothing, yet."

"But—"

"Colonel Cody could have hidden his gun or had someone take it to establish an alibi."

"No," Dooley insisted.

Wiggins put a hand on Dooley's shoulder, trying to calm his friend.

"What makes you so sure?" Desmond inquired.

"We're not," Jennie replied. "It's just that Colonel Cody wouldn't have any reason to attack that constable."

"Perhaps, young lady," Desmond mused. "Or rather, he has no reason we know about. But there could be some little secret the colonel and his Indian friends are hiding."

Wiggins and the others quickly exchanged glances.

"Whatever is going on, we'll ferret it out." Desmond leaned a bit closer to them. "But you young people should stay out of it, please." He gave each of them a long, steady look. "I wouldn't want what happened to the constable to happen to you."

Chapter 5

BEFORE ANY OF THE RAVEN LEAGUE COULD RESPOND to Desmond's serious words, the inspector stepped to the edge of the pavement and hailed a passing hansom cab. In moments, the two-wheeled cab was rattling away over the cobblestones.

Wiggins's shoulders sagged, and it wasn't just from the thought of the long walk home.

"I don't know which is more annoying," Jennie complained. "The way he treated us as if we hadn't a brain in our heads or having him say the gun being stolen earlier didn't matter."

"At least the coppers aren't just looking at Buffalo Bill," Owens said. "It sounds as if they'll be picking on the Indians he brought with him, though."

"What would you expect them to do after some fellow has his hair lifted?" Wiggins asked.

"Perhaps," Jennie admitted. "But there's no proof that they did it."

"Well, I hope they lock up those savages," Dooley said. "Then they can't hurt anyone else."

"More likely, they'll just keep an eye on them." Wiggins scratched his head.

"I wish I could stay on with you," Dooley said. "But my da is supposed to get off work on the docks early today. We're going to have a meal and all."

"I ought to be going too," Jennie added. "There should be some sewing work I can pick up to take home to Mother."

After quick good-byes, Dooley and Jennie set off. Owens gave Wiggins a sidelong look. "You're not going to let it go, are you?"

"Maybe I should," Wiggins replied. "Maybe I should just be glad like Dooley and let the coppers go after the savages. What do I owe them? But then I remember the Indian who calmed down the buffalo outside the show."

"Silent Eagle." Owens shrugged. "All he did was bring some grain."

"Would you walk up to a giant beast that was huffing and puffing away? One false move and it could have turned Silent Eagle into jelly—along with us, I'd wager. That took courage."

Owens shrugged again. "As much as you'd need to slice a man's hair off?" he asked. "Maybe he's the Indian who attacked the constable."

"That copper was already wounded. He couldn't have stopped whoever scalped him," Wiggins replied. "His attacker wasn't brave. He was a coward."

Owens slowly nodded. "So, I say we go to the exhibition grounds and nose around some more."

Moving southwest, the boys hitched rides on the backs of wagons and carriages until they jumped off only a short walk from the exhibition grounds.

"I hope you've been thinking up some sort of plan on the way here," Owens said as they got closer to the exposition. "Do you plan to tell the ticket taker we're personal friends of Buffalo Bill?" He grinned. "Or do we hope they're moving another buffalo in?"

Wiggins didn't have a plan, but as they arrived at the exhibition grounds, they quickly saw that wouldn't have mattered. All bridges leading to the show grounds—and to the tent village—were guarded by groups of police constables.

"What are they all doing here?" Owens asked.

Wiggins sighed. "We heard Mr. Pryke shooting his mouth off to Inspector Desmond about Americans in general—and the Wild West show folk in particular. I'll bet he's been stirring up others as well. Maybe it would be a good idea to keep people out."

Owens abruptly nudged him. "There are a couple of familiar folks."

Wiggins quickly spotted a short figure in a dapper suit talking with a taller, bronze-skinned figure in rough clothes. "Nate Salsbury and Silent Eagle," he said.

Even from a distance, Wiggins could see that the two men clearly weren't having a friendly chat. At last, Salsbury abruptly turned away and walked off through the police guards. When Silent Eagle went to follow, the constables turned him back. The Indian vanished into the tented area.

"Looks as if the idea is to keep *some* people in," Owens said in a dry voice.

"Just yesterday, you were carrying on about the way Indians scalped people," Wiggins growled. "Is it any wonder the coppers would be suspicious?"

"Buffalo Bill took some scalps too," Owens replied. "I wonder if the coppers are keeping *him* in?"

There was no way to answer that, just as there was nothing they could do here. As the boys turned away, however, Wiggins caught a hint of movement from the corner of the lot where the performers' tents stood. He spotted a human figure drop from the top of the wall that enclosed the Wild West show area. The man slid down the steep embankment to the railway tracks, where he disappeared from the boys' sight. Seconds later, he swung himself over the top of the fence on their side of the tracks, dropping lightly to the pavement.

The boys looked toward the nearest group of policemen. Obviously, they'd noticed nothing. Wiggins and Owens stared as the escaping man paused to tuck long, black hair under a scruffy hat. He ran off, but there was no mistaking the hawk-like face they'd seen—it was Silent Eagle.

The question was, what was he up to?

Evening was coming on by the time the boys got back to the East End. Wiggins could feel a strange kind of energy in the neighborhood even before he spotted teams of men slapping large handbills on every space they could find.

It took both boys working together to figure out the words on the top line of the handbill. "'Monster rally,'" Wiggins said finally. But there was a lot more to decipher.

"I think we may need to show this to Jennie," Owens said.

After glancing to see that the handbill crew had moved along, Wiggins yanked down the still-damp paper.

"So . . . let's find her," he said.

They checked several places before finding Jennie at the Raven Pub. She sat grim-faced in the back room, Dooley at her side, an evening newspaper spread before them.

"Da ended up working late after all." Dooley tried to hide his disappointment with a smile. "Then on the way home, I heard the newsboys—"

"And I bought another paper." Jennie thumped a hand down on the newsprint. "Somehow, our friend Mr. Pryke must have gotten a look at Inspector

Desmond's report from the hospital. According to this newspaper, he's accusing Buffalo Bill of smuggling, bringing savages into Britain, attacking people . . . just about everything but trying to overthrow the Crown."

"Give him time," Owens said.

Wiggins produced the handbill they'd taken down. "I suppose that's what this is all about."

Jennie looked it over. "It's not as long-winded as the things he told the newspaper reporters, but otherwise it's about the same. Smuggling. No respect for law. Savage behavior. And he's inviting everyone to a mass meeting to discuss it tonight."

Wiggins picked up the handbill. "Then that's where we should be."

Just after nightfall, crowds of men appeared, whooping it up and waving burning torches as they marched through the East End. They congregated for the meeting in Stepney, at an open area called Arbour Square. Wiggins and the other members of the Raven League followed their friends and neighbors. Most of the people around them seemed to treat the proceedings as a sort of holiday, laughing and larking about.

"I don't see any of our folks here," Wiggins observed.

"You won't catch my ma at one of these," Owens replied. "Pryke doesn't spend much time in the West Indian and Hindu neighborhoods. Guess he's not 'one of *us*.'"

Wiggins caught sight of a familiar figure standing at the edge of the growing crowd. He nudged Owens. "Isn't that your friend Mr. Shears?"

Shears was a local barber who'd served in the army with Owens's father. After the older Owens had died in battle, Shears had befriended the whole Owens family. Right now, he stood with his hands on his hips, looking as if he'd just tasted a particularly sour persimmon.

"Mr. Shears!" Owens said as they came closer. "What brings you out here?"

His smile of greeting dimmed a bit. "I came to hear what that *fellow* has to say." From the look on the barber's face, Wiggins knew Mr. Shears had wanted to call Pryke some other name.

"I knew Jemmy Pryke when he had a rathole of an office, earning a dubious living by trying to keep burglars from going to prison," Shears said. "Then all of a sudden he was standing for Parliament as 'J. Montague Pryke, friend of the working man.'"

Shears shook his head. "His whole life, he was just a mouth working for whoever crossed his palm with silver. That's what he's still doing, though I don't know where the money comes from."

Jennie frowned. "You think someone is paying for all this?"

"Could be." Mr. Shears shrugged. "Sometimes he does this to make himself look important. East Enders are Pryke's favorite audience. Folk round here are poor enough—ignorant enough—angry enough—to swallow his kind of 'oratory.'"

J. Montague Pryke began his speech. He started off sounding reasonable. But his voice began to rise as he called up every argument the British had had with their American cousins since the colonies broke away in 1776. Americans, it seemed, were just naturally greedy, crude, and treacherous in general. And when it came to Buffalo Bill and his performers in particular, Pryke painted an even worse picture. Colonel Cody and the cowboys represented some sort of nasty subhumans not fit to live in decent society. The Indians were even worse.

"They're a degenerate race that refuses to be civilized and that treats civilized folk with the utmost savagery," Pryke shouted. "But when this Yankee brings his freak show to London—to the center of world civilization—what happens? Thirty to forty thousand people pack each performance. He dines with the finest in the land and sends millions back to America. Is this right?"

Faces red, eyes bulging, torches shaking, the crowd shouted, "NO!"

"But is Cody content? No! He unleashes his pet savages on the very symbol of decent, civilized London life—one of the honest bobbies who work to protect us all. Will we stand for this?"

For Wiggins, like most East Enders, the less he had to do with the coppers, the better. But now, his neighbors were ready to die for this injured constable. *And I'd be yelling right beside them,* he realized with some embarrassment, *except I met Buffalo Bill and saw what sort of man he is. I saw Silent Eagle risk his life calming that buffalo to save a crowd of people he didn't even know—people who would mock him as an ignorant savage.*

He looked to see his friends' reactions. Jennie's lips were tight. "My friend Jacob told me stories about meetings like this in Russia," she said. "Afterward, the people took their torches to burn down the Jewish part of town."

"Happens here too," Owens added grimly.

Wiggins didn't know what to say to that, so he turned away. Then he froze, staring.

Owens noticed. "What is it?"

Wiggins jerked his head off to the left. "I recognize someone over there. Natty Blount." Natty had been a pickpocket when Wiggins brought him into the Baker Street Irregulars, the boys who did odd jobs for Sherlock Holmes. But he became another kind of thief, stealing control of the Irregulars from Wiggins. Owens's hand tightened on Wiggins's shoulder as he spotted Blount not twenty feet from them, waving a torch and yelling his head off.

Seeing the petty thief who had wrecked the Baker Street Irregulars filled Wiggins with familiar anger—and sudden suspicion. He began searching the crowd for other faces he knew.

They were easy enough to spot—shorter figures, all of them waving torches. Once they had been Sherlock Holmes's eyes and ears all over London. Now they were just another gang of street toughs. They cared nothing for politics or patriotism, just cold, hard cash. If they were here, they were here for money and no other reason.

"Pryke ain't alone in whipping up the crowd,"

Wiggins told the others. "He's got a mob for hire helping him."

Jennie's eyebrows drew together. "I wonder what that means?"

Wiggins and Owens exchanged worried looks. "It means," Wiggins said slowly, "that someone is out to cause trouble for Colonel Cody and the Americans."

Chapter 6

"ARCHIBALD WIGGINS! WHERE ARE YOU GOING?"
Wiggins's mother stood in the doorway of their
rooms, her hands on her hips and a grim expression on her face. "I've been baking all night. The
least you could do is deliver these orders for me this
morning."

"I know, Mam," Wiggins replied sheepishly. "But
I have to meet the lads—uh, Jennie and the others.
Something important has—"

"Not so important that you can slack off on your
chores around here."

"But—"

His mother raised a disapproving eyebrow, and
the corners of her lips curled down. It was a look
that Wiggins knew too well. His mother would tol-
erate no more debate. Selling her baked goods was
their only source of income since Wiggins's father

had died. Wiggins knew that the little money he made running errands for other people did not amount to much. Not even his work for Mr. Sherlock Holmes excluded him from helping her when she needed him.

Wiggins trotted back up the stairs and into their room. "Sorry, Mam," he said with an apologetic grin. "Where did you want me to deliver those goodies?"

The two errands didn't really take too long. As he jogged along the cobblestone streets toward the last shopkeeper, Wiggins realized that the small detour was actually useful to him.

Everywhere he looked, Wiggins saw handbills posted up by Pryke's supporters. Here and there, small groups of agitated people stood reading the handbills and discussing the message.

Though Wiggins couldn't read them himself, he gathered from the others that the bills spoke angrily against what they called an American "infestation." They even suggested that the London constabulary was coddling people of prestige and influence.

Wiggins shook his head with disgust. Like Mr. Holmes, he had never cared much about politics.

All the titles and speeches were just so much noise to him. But after the Raven League's first adventure, Wiggins had begun to put faces to the names in government. After all, he'd met the queen of England. He'd also met assassins and learned that there were spies—even in the British government.

Winding his way toward the Raven Pub, Wiggins continued to think about the case at hand. If someone was out to hurt Buffalo Bill and his show, or any Americans, they might be planning to use East Enders to do their dirty work. And later, when the law demanded justice, it would be the East Enders who would pay.

If that was the case, what could he and the League do to stop them? The last time they'd had Sherlock Holmes on their side. Should they go to the detective?

Wiggins reached a decision when he finally met up with Jennie and the others in the back room of the Raven Pub.

"You're late," Jennie scolded. "What kept you?"

"I'll explain along the way," Wiggins replied. "Right now, we're paying a call on Buffalo Bill. I got his address, but we have a ways to go."

In a few minutes, the four were hurrying west-ward along Mile End Road. Wiggins quickly told them about the handbills and what he had heard.

"Yeah," Dooley said, nodding in agreement. "I was out early shining shoes of folks going to work. I heard them talking about this all morning long."

"I heard the same from the roughs hanging about the streets," Wiggins added. "They're saying Cody and the other savages should leave London." He glanced over at Owens, who hadn't cracked a joke or made a comment. "Have you heard anything?"

Owens nodded but didn't look at Wiggins. "Even some of my people are calling the Americans all sorts of names."

"That bothers you?" Dooley asked.

Owens shrugged. "Seems funny. We don't want no one treatin' us like dirt, but we're quick to do it to others."

Wiggins pointed toward the back of a large fur-niture wagon rattling along the street. "There's our ride."

The others caught on and one by one ran behind the vehicle to jump onto the tailgate of the wagon.

"I still think that mob at Pryke's speech last night was bought," Wiggins proclaimed after they were all aboard. "Nat Blount was there, and he doesn't care anything about people—except the ones he plans to nick something from. Same for some of those blokes he was standing with."

"Maybe he was trying to pick a few pockets in the crowd," Owens offered.

"If he went after one of those blokes he was standing with," Wiggins shot back, "they'd have hacked off his fingers and fed them to him one by one."

"What would be the purpose of hiring a phony crowd of angry citizens?" Jennie asked.

"Maybe to make Pryke look important," Wiggins replied.

"But he's already important," Jennie said.

"This is getting too mixed up for me." Dooley shook his head. "Are we after thugs, smugglers, or what?"

"I have no idea," Wiggins admitted, then he went quiet. The wagon rattled along westward to Piccadilly, where Wiggins signaled for them to get ready to hop off.

"Well, once we figure out who took Buffalo Bill's gun, we'll have the answer." Wiggins dropped from the wagon, and the others followed.

He took a quick glance around to get his bearings. This neighborhood was expensive, near the fine gentlemen's clubs and the theaters. Coming up to Regent Street, he led the way to number 59.

They stood in front of the five-story stone building, whose ground floor was a gentleman's outfitters. "Colonel Cody has two floors of rooms upstairs, or so this mate of mine told me," Wiggins said. "He helped deliver some of the flowers all the ladies were sending to Buffalo Bill."

A four-wheeled coach waited out in the street, and the front door of the house stood partially open.

While the coach driver was distracted by his horse, Wiggins walked up to the house and gingerly gave the doorknob a pull. The door swung farther open. "In we go," he said.

Jennie sent a worried glance at the coach's driver, but he never glanced at the children as they entered the house.

Wiggins went to peer up the stairway while the others huddled together by a large potted palm—almost as if they thought they'd blend in with the foliage.

"Come on," Wiggins whispered over his shoulder.

He turned back to discover a stocky man in a derby hat frowning up above them. "Where did you lot come from? This is a gentleman's establishment. No casual labor or mendicants need apply."

"It's the butler." Owens took a nervous step back.

"Not fancy enough." Wiggins smirked. "He's probably a valet."

"Do I need to repeat myself?" the servant said sharply. "We don't allow beggars in here."

"We ain't beggars," Wiggins told him. "We're here to see Buffalo—I mean, Colonel Cody."

"Yeah, we're friends of his," Dooley added.

"Of course you are." The servant pushed back his sleeves as he came down the steps toward the children. "Since you won't leave nicely, I'll just have to—"

"Now wait just a minute, guv." Wiggins threw up his hands to fend off the man's grip.

"You touch me," Dooley warned loudly, "and I'll take—"

"What's going on here, Jim?"

A new figure appeared at the head of the stairs: Buffalo Bill's partner, Nate Salsbury.

"I was just about to evict them, sir," Jim said anxiously. He'd managed to snag both Jennie and Wiggins by their collars.

"Hello, Mr. Salsbury," Jennie said politely. Wiggins wanted to laugh at the sight of Jennie trying to maintain her dignity as the servant gripped her collar. "It's good to see you again."

"Hello again, little missy," Salsbury replied with a wry smile.

"You know these—children?" the servant asked.

"They were visiting Colonel Cody in his tent," the show manager said as he approached the group. "Let 'em go."

As the servant moved away with a dazed expression on his face, Dooley stuck his tongue out at the man. But when the servant glanced back at the group, Dooley appeared to be studying the design on the rug.

"If you came by to enjoy Colonel Cody's hospitality," Salsbury told them, "you've picked a bad time."

"Why?" Owens asked.

"Surely you've heard about the attack," Salsbury replied. "I was here with Bill last night

when the police came around to question us again."
He gazed back up the stairs.

"We read about it," Wiggins said, "and we
thought of something that might help."

Salsbury turned back around to face them.
"What do you know that might help us?"

"The newspapers—and other people—are
making a lot of the fact that the gun found by the
constable belonged to Buffalo Bill," Wiggins said.
"But we know it was lost long before the attack.
Remember?"

"Lost," Jennie echoed, "or stolen."

"Well, look who we've got here!" a loud voice
interrupted.

"Hi, Buffalo Bill!" Dooley almost cheered
as the frontiersman walked down the stairs and
joined them.

"Morning," Cody said, ruffling Dooley's hair
and shaking hands with the others. "What brings
you here?"

Jennie quickly explained the reason for their
visit. "Did you ever find out how the gun got out of
your tent?"

Cody shook his head. "Nate and I looked
into it."

"You may find it hard to believe, considering your visit," Salsbury told them with a grin. "But very few people have access to the tent during the show."

Cody shrugged. "I can't see any of my folks stealing one of my guns. They had plenty of opportunities before, and nothing like this has ever happened."

"I think it was some souvenir hunter," Salsbury said, "and I'll say as much to Inspector Desmond the next time I see him." He shook his head. "I doubt, though, that will be enough for the local police—or the newspapers. They'll still suggest that Cody or someone else in the show hid the gun, pretending that he'd lost it."

"It would have to be a pretty determined souvenir hunter if no one could get into that area," Wiggins said. "And why would he attack the copper?"

"The police are determined to prove that one of my people took the gun and then turned it against the policeman," Cody said. "It's up to me, not you young ones, to prove otherwise. After all, a man was scalped."

"*Shot* and scalped," Owens added.

"Not with my gun," Cody said firmly. "It was loaded with blanks, like all the guns in the show."

"Are you sure?" Wiggins asked.

Colonel Cody nodded. "Only two shots had been fired. The other cartridges were still in the gun. They were blanks, all right."

"That explains it!" Jennie exclaimed. "The newspapers said the constable had been shot. But the doctor at St. Bartholomew's said there was no gunshot wound."

Wiggins was trying to decide what to make of that when Dooley cried, "We'll help you sort this out, Colonel Cody!"

"And we know a person who may be even more helpful," Jennie said. "Mr. Sherlock Holmes."

She had taken the words right out of Wiggins's mouth. However, he noticed that Nate Salsbury seemed to tense on hearing the great detective's name.

"We don't need anyone else nosing about in this," Salsbury said. "To be honest, we've been trying to lie low. The last thing we need is more unfriendly attention from the newspapers. Our publicity man is having nightmares as it is."

Colonel Cody put a steadying hand on Salsbury's shoulder. "Nate's a little wound up right now," he said. "But I say whoever attacked and scalped that policeman needs to be caught and taught a lesson."

"But Colonel—"

"But nothing, Nate," Cody interrupted. "My reputation means a lot to me, but the lives of the people in the show mean more. I think we can use any help we can get. So if Mr. Holmes can take the case, I'd be glad of it."

"Then we'll speak to him for you," Wiggins said, proud to be able to make the offer.

"Well, thank you kindly," Colonel Cody replied. "Since you're working for me, seems only fair that you should be pulling a salary."

The frontiersman reached into his pocket and pulled out a handful of coins. "I'm still not all that certain of how your money works, but this should be enough to start."

Wiggins and the others stared in wide-eyed amazement as Colonel Cody poured crowns, shillings, and pence into Wiggins's hands.

"That's almost two pounds there," Dooley gasped.

Cody took out a card and scribbled on it. "This will get you into the show grounds whenever you need to bring any messages." He grinned. "What's the matter? Not enough?"

"Oh, more than enough," Wiggins said enthusiastically. "And don't worry, we do this all the time. Getting Mr. Holmes to help will be no problem at all."

"What do you mean, he's not home?" Owens exclaimed in dismay.

The young girl in the ill-fitting maid's uniform stood in the doorway of 221B Baker Street like a grenadier guard at Buckingham Palace. "I mean," she replied, "that he and Dr. Watson ain't here," she said, sounding annoyed. "They're away on business."

Dooley stepped forward, a smile on his face and a twinkle in his eye. "You remember me, don't you?" he asked her. "You helped me, uh, us the last time we were here."

The girl looked around nervously. "I remember," she replied. "But Mrs. Hudson could be back at any minute, and I ain't supposed to let anyone—"

"Could you at least tell us when Mr. Holmes will be back?" Dooley asked her.

"Not really." The girl continued to glance up and down the street. "They left this morning for King's Cross Station, but Mr. Holmes said they was flyin'."

"Flyin'?" Owens repeated blankly.

"Did they take anything?" Wiggins asked.

"Each of 'em had a Gladstone bag. Now I have to go!" With that, the young maid quickly shut the door.

"How can anyone—" Jennie began.

Wiggins smiled at the look on her face. "They ain't *flying*," he explained. "They're taking the *Flying* Scotsman. It's a train that leaves from King's Cross, going all the way up to Edinburgh."

"Scotland—and bags," Owens moaned. "They could be gone for days."

Dooley removed his cap and scratched his fiery red hair. "Just grand, that is. What do we do now?"

Wiggins tried to recall how Mr. Holmes had used the Irregulars. What would he have assigned them to do now? The image of Nat Blount flashed before his eyes, waving a torch at Pryke's rally. Suddenly, Wiggins had a plan.

"Follow me." Wiggins led the group down Baker Street, heading for the Underground station.

"Someone tries to frame Colonel Cody," Wiggins began slowly as the idea took shape. "And right away,

Pryke starts making all Americans look bad. Maybe those things are connected."

"You mean because Colonel Cody is an American, Mr. Pryke might have tried to frame him?" Jennie asked.

"Why not?" Wiggins said.

"But how do we find out if that's true?" Owens asked.

"By checking on Nat Blount and his friends from the mob last night." Wiggins fished out some money as they approached the Underground train station. "I say Nat was hired to be part of that mob, so he might lead us to who hired him."

"So let's get looking for the little rat," Owens said.

Wiggins held up his hands. "There's something else. What did you think about Mr. Salsbury?"

"He was nice enough," Jennie said. "But . . . distracted."

"He wasn't happy when you mentioned Mr. Holmes." Dooley scowled in memory. "And he was mean to that Indian."

Wiggins's eyebrows rose as he remembered what seemed to have been an argument between the two Wild West employees. Was that why Silent

Eagle had snuck off the grounds? Was he following Salsbury?

"Mr. Salsbury also didn't seem too interested about who could have taken Buffalo Bill's gun," Jennie said. "Maybe that's because *he's* the thief."

"You think *he* took Buffalo Bill's gun?" Owens asked. "Why? So he could make his partner look bad?"

"Maybe Salsbury wants to run the show," Jennie said. "Or maybe he wants to sell the gun to some souvenir collector. Perhaps I'll go around to the pawnshops. Pawnbrokers often deal with collectors." She colored. "Mother and I have become familiar with some pawnbrokers lately."

"All right, then," Wiggins said, mulling over the possibilities. "See what you and Dooley can find out while Owens and I go look for Natty Blount. We'll all meet again here at the Raven."

Wiggins and Owens scoured the East End looking for Natty Blount—with no luck.

"Just grand," Wiggins complained. "All the time I don't want to see him, he turns up like a bad penny."

Just then, Owens nudged him with an elbow. "Keep

walking," the other boy said, looking straight ahead. "But turn your eyes a little bit to your left."

Without turning his head, Wiggins did as he was asked. A sly smile appeared on his lips. Across the street was a building both of them knew— the gaming club that a gang leader named Limehouse Lew had used for his headquarters. Lew was no more, but his chief lieutenant, a big bruiser named Alfie Sinnott, had kept the business going. Today, Sinnott stood out on the doorstep as a line stretched down the block. Each bloke came by with his hand outstretched. Sinnott dropped a coin into each palm— including Natty Blount's.

As Wiggins walked along, trying not to call attention to himself, he counted four other people he'd seen last night waving torches. He grabbed Owens by the arm and almost ran around the corner.

"Well, we don't need to talk to Natty now." Wiggins couldn't keep the grin off his face. "We got what we came for."

They ran back to the Raven Pub, eager to report their success. Jennie and Dooley were already in the back room when Wiggins popped in, shouting, "You won't believe what we just saw!"

He stopped short when he saw the glum looks on their faces. "What's the matter? You couldn't get a sniff about Buffalo Bill's gun?"

"It's what we just heard out in the public room." Jennie's voice was tight. "Mr. Pryke was found horribly beaten. They say he could die!"

Wiggins stared. "Is there anything to show who did it?"

Jennie nodded miserably. "He was holding something in his hand. A porcupine quill from America, tied in a piece of buckskin decorated with purple glass beads."

"That's the sort of thing you'd find on an Indian costume," Dooley said. "Now even the people who don't like Pryke are seein' red—and the red they want to see is Indian blood."

Chapter 7

"THINGS JUST KEEP GETTING BETTER AND BETTER, don't they?" Owens tried to sound lighthearted, but he couldn't hide the worry in his eyes.

Wiggins jammed his hands in his pockets. "First thing tomorrow, we're going out to the exhibition grounds."

"Last time you tried that, there were a lot of coppers around," Dooley pointed out.

"But now we have a note from Buffalo Bill, don't we?" Wiggins said. "That should get us in."

Dooley brightened a little but still looked doubtful. "What will we do when we get there?"

"We'll nose around," Wiggins said. "Just like the Irregulars did for Mr. Holmes—keeping our ears open."

"We should talk to the Indians and see if anyone has a costume with those quills," Jennie began.

"I'm not going near them." Dooley jumped up, his eyes bright with fear. "'Specially that Silent Eagle gink."

"He can't scalp us just for asking," Owens joked.

"How will we get to Earl's Court?" Jennie continued to concentrate on problems.

"We'll manage," Wiggins said. "Just wear something you won't mind getting dusty."

They broke up, and Wiggins headed for home. Maybe he had sounded confident, but his head fairly buzzed as he tried to make sense of this new development. Could Silent Eagle, or one of the other Indians working for Buffalo Bill, have attacked the loud-mouthed Pryke? The decoration in the politician's hand certainly suggested that. But then, it would also suggest that Pryke's attacker had been dressed as a warrior.

Wiggins had a sudden mental picture of Silent Eagle stealing out of the performers' camp. *Still*, he thought, *it's one thing to sneak past a few coppers. It's another to cross London dressed up in feathers and beads.*

Nonetheless, he had a bad feeling about all of this—and he feared things were only going to get worse.

*　　*　　*

The next morning, they made their way to the Earl's Court exhibition grounds, stealing a ride at the tail of a wagon.

Soon enough, they reached the exhibition grounds. Jennie moved to the front of the group as they came to the bridge leading to the covered grandstand and the performers' encampment. Approaching the police guards, she thrust out the note from Buffalo Bill.

Wiggins hung behind, having spotted the ruddy face of Benny Flagg. Benny drove a hansom cab, but he'd unhitched his horse just past the bridge that led to the corral area. A row of stables for the horses in the Wild West show stood there. The cabbie shook his head as Wiggins came up.

"Hoped one of the stable blokes might come over to help." Benny gently touched a large, inflamed sore spot on the horse's shoulder, getting an unhappy snort in reply. "Harness gall," Flagg said gloomily. "The old nag ain't going to pull this rig. The RSPCA people would pinch me, just like that copper that went inside aims to do."

"Copper?" Wiggins repeated.

"Yeah, the one who dresses like a gent, with his mustache clipped just so." Flagg had described Inspector Desmond in a quick sentence. "He came with two men to arrest one of the Indians."

When Wiggins heard that, he dashed to the other bridge to catch up with his friends. He saw that the constables set on guard had formed a cordon at the far end of the bridge, locking their arms together. On the far side of the police line stood at least fifty stone-faced Indians, some equally grim cowboys—and Jennie, Owens, and Dooley.

Inspector Desmond stepped onto the bridge, a pair of constables behind him and a handcuffed Indian between them—Silent Eagle. Angry-looking young Indians came forward, only to be waved back by a chief in a feathered warbonnet.

I can see why they're upset, Wiggins thought, *but they really seem to have something against the coppers.* A thought suddenly flashed across his mind. In their blue uniforms and flat hats, the British coppers resembled pictures he'd seen of the blue-coated U.S. cavalry who'd fought the Indians in the past. Many of the warriors looked ready to have a go at this thin blue line here and now.

Desmond and his prisoner had nearly reached Wiggins on the other side of the bridge when another mob appeared from around the American Exposition building. Apparently, this crowd had just arrived from a nearby train station. The men had the shabby clothes and the gray, unwashed faces of classic East End loafers. Judging from the angry looks and waving fists, Wiggins figured they had decided to get busy today and the reason, he realized with a sinking heart, was obvious.

"There that savage is!" someone at the head of the mob shouted. "He's the one wot done for Mr. Pryke!"

The low growl from the mob sounded as vicious as anything that Wiggins had ever heard. He glanced down the street, where Benny Flagg still stood, then back to the line of police, trying to figure out which way to go. In a moment, Wiggins ran out of choices. The mob surged forward, shouting, aiming to seal off the bridge.

Wiggins retreated until he stood beside Desmond. The police inspector raised both arms, waving the crowd back. "This man is in police custody," he shouted in the very voice of authority. "He will be taken to Scotland Yard and, in due course, will face a British jury."

For a moment, Wiggins thought that Desmond's calm approach might just defuse the situation. Crowd members began backing away, opening a path.

Then someone in the mob shouted, "To blazes with that! We come all this way, we'll take care of 'im!"

Wiggins had no doubt that "taking care" of Silent Eagle meant something very bad indeed. Maybe even something deadly.

A knot of mob members, angrier—or drunker—than the rest, suddenly rushed forward. Among them was a big bruiser who confronted one of the constables accompanying Desmond. The copper tried to pull out his baton, but a single blow from a massive fist ended things quickly. The police officer dropped senseless at Silent Eagle's feet.

Instantly, the Wild West performers burst into shouts, pushing against the line of constables.

Wiggins figured the Indian stood no chance if the mob members got their hands on him. Silent Eagle must have reached the same conclusion. His foot came up, lashing out in a kick to the big man's belly. The oversized attacker went from loudly cheering his success to fighting for breath, clutching his middle as he folded in half.

Silent Eagle brought up his manacled hands, clasped together into one fist, clouting the gasping man on the side of the head. The big man spun and fell down, bringing three mob members down with him.

Taking advantage of the suddenly created open space, Silent Eagle dashed forward, using the man he'd just felled as a sort of springboard—launching off his back in a leap toward the thinnest part of the astonished crowd.

"Constables! After him!" Inspector Desmond roared to the police who'd been blocking off the other end of the bridge. As his men ran after Silent Eagle, the Wild West performers broke through the police line and stormed onto the bridge. The whole scene became a wild melee as the three groups clashed together.

Wiggins dodged and ducked punches and truncheons, trying to keep an eye on Silent Eagle's escape.

"Cor!" Wiggins exclaimed. Silent Eagle showed all the Indian bravery, strength, and ruthlessness that Wiggins expected. The man used knees, elbows, and even his bound wrists as a club to fight his way to freedom.

Silent Eagle tore his way clear of the lynch mob and ran straight to where Benny Flagg stood trying to calm down his cab horse, spooked by the noise and fighting.

Snatching the reins from the cabbie, Silent Eagle vaulted onto the horse's back. It would be hard to tell which was more dumbfounded, Benny or his horse.

The animal reared, lashing out with his fore-hooves, and the pursuing mob backed up hastily.

Wiggins was sure Silent Eagle would fall off the rearing horse, but the warrior clung to his mount as if he'd become a part of the beast, turning it around.

He might make it, Wiggins thought, *if he could only get his hands free. . . .*

He glanced over at the police officer who'd been downed at the beginning of the riot. The man still lay unconscious on the cobblestones. Hanging from his belt, Wiggins caught the glitter of keys.

Bobbing and weaving, Wiggins made his way through the struggling mass of people. He dropped to one knee and tore loose the key ring. Hunched over, he barreled his way to the end of the bridge and some open space.

With all his might, he flung the keys toward the fleeing Indian.

Even as he did so, a voice jeered inside his head. *Fool,* it said. *Even if he sees them, what is he going to do? Stop, get down, and pick them up?*

Silent Eagle apparently *did* see the keys because the horse veered in their direction. However, the Indian didn't rein in his galloping mount. Instead he swung around, clinging with one leg as he stretched to the pavement.

Wiggins shuddered, certain the bareback rider would tumble to the hard stones and break his neck. But an instant later, Silent Eagle pulled himself upright, keys held victoriously aloft in his upraised hands.

Seconds later, both Indian and cab horse left the fighting and screaming behind, clattering out of sight.

Chapter 8

WIGGINS DIDN'T SEE WHAT HAPPENED NEXT. SOME-
one tripped over him, and they both wound up
on the pavement. All he heard were cries of anger and pain, pierced with the shrill tweets of
police whistles as officers called for more assistance.

By the time Wiggins regained his feet, Silent
Eagle was long gone. Members of the angry
mob were chasing him on foot, though they had
no chance of catching him.

Wiggins watched as several constables struggled to hold back a knot of cowboys and Indians.
Some were cheering Silent Eagle's escape, while
others were yelling back at members of the thin-
ning mob. Another detachment of constables
rushed to subdue that bunch.

Through all the chaos, Wiggins spotted Inspector Desmond shouting orders to some of the policemen. The Scotland Yard detective was covered in grime. His hair was mussed, and his tie had been half torn loose.

Desmond's expression was hard as he mopped his face with a handkerchief. He glanced with distaste at the stains on the linen and crumpled it into his pocket. Then he noticed Wiggins.

"Were you part of this madness?" Desmond asked, his hands curling into fists at his sides.

"Course not," Wiggins protested. "I was trying to get away when that mob cut me off."

"Perhaps that's true," the inspector replied slowly. "But I find it strange how you are always around when something happens."

Wiggins was about to reply when he saw Jennie appear from the dispersing crowd and push past a constable. The police were gaining control of the mob. They had arrested some, but most of the people were being told to go home or simply leave the area.

"Wiggins!" Jennie called out. "Are you all right?"

Wiggins nodded. "Yes. Where are Owens and Dooley?"

Jennie was about to answer him when she noticed Inspector Desmond glaring at them. "I don't know," she replied. "We all got jostled apart."

Desmond leaned forward. "Why are *any* of you here at all?"

"We heard about the attack on Mr. Pryke and about the Indian quill they found," Wiggins explained. "We thought we could help. Maybe find out who's really doing all of this."

"We even talked to Colonel Cody about his missing gun," Jennie added. "And he—"

"Scotland Yard doesn't need your assistance," Desmond told them. His tone was hard and authoritative. "We have matters under control, and hardly need street Arabs to do our work for us."

Wiggins gazed off in the direction Silent Eagle had escaped. "Didn't look that way a while ago," he said.

"That's because some *other* citizens did not mind their own affairs," the inspector replied harshly.

"We had nothing to do with that mob," Jennie insisted. "Or Silent Eagle's escape."

Wiggins pressed his lips together. *If she only knew*, he told himself.

"We're just trying to help," Jennie concluded.

"Your participation in this matter ends here," the inspector told them. He glanced toward the still-cheering Wild West performers, then back at the two children. "We're hunting a brutal man, and anyone who aids him will find themselves in a cell right next to him."

Desmond stalked off to join the other policemen.

Jennie stood fuming. "You'd think we were criminals, the way he treated us," she said.

"Well, maybe one of us is . . . kind of," Wiggins said.

"What do you mean?" Jennie asked.

"I'll explain while we look for Owens and Dooley," Wiggins replied. "Come on."

Owens and Dooley stood staring at the collection of tents stretching ahead of them. They'd passed this way before but hadn't noticed much. Their eyes had been on Buffalo Bill. Now they saw that the larger tents nearby seemed to be some sort of offices for the show. A friendly cowboy had pointed out the Indian tepees.

"I never seen nothing like this in my whole life," Dooley said. He was a quivering collection of awe and fear as he cautiously entered the Indians' territory.

"My dad used to sleep under tents—him being in the army and all." Owens tried to sound as if there was nothing unusual about wandering through a tent community. "My mum told me stories about how she and some of her family used to sleep outside sometimes."

"In the streets?"

"No." Owens shook his head. "When she lived in the West Indies. Before she met my dad and came here."

"Well, I bet it wasn't nothing like this," Dooley replied. "Look at all these savages."

Owens bristled. "I wish you'd stop calling them that."

"Why?" Dooley asked in surprise.

"I begin to think they're sick of hearing it," Owens said, "like folks calling me 'golliwog.' How do you feel when someone calls a lie 'Irish testimony'?"

Dooley stared at Owens openmouthed, then turned to look out at the scene before them. "You think Wiggins and Jennie are all right?" he asked, changing the subject. "Maybe we shouldn't have left them when the mob showed up."

"They can take care of themselves," Owens replied. "And it was our best chance to get round here. Now . . ." He looked around until he found the largest tepee on the grounds. "The cowboy we spoke to said that Chief Red Shirt was with Buffalo Bill?"

"Yeah," Dooley replied. "He said they'd gone off to meet with some important people."

"Probably trying to convince them that the Indians aren't evil." Owens smiled.

"But"—Dooley pulled his cap down lower over his hair—"he did say we could talk to Chief Tall-Like-Oak, and that he'd be in—"

"The tent with the target and stars," Owens interrupted, pointing. "Well, there she is, although I think that's supposed to be the moon, not a target."

Owens led Dooley over to the cone-shaped structure. The animal skin that served as a door was off to one side, and the boys could see a lone figure sitting on a blanket beside a small fire.

"What's this made out of—leather?" Dooley poked at the taut body of the tent, stretched over thin wooden poles.

"Don't know." Owens hesitated at the entrance, feeling as if going into the tent would be entering another world, the world of the alien figure sitting inside. Tiny beads of sweat formed on his forehead. "So . . . let's go ask him."

Owens poked his head into the tent. "Excuse me," he said politely. "Are you Chief Tall-Like-Oak?"

The Indian studied Owens before he replied with a nod. "The show does not start for another hour," he told them.

"We didn't come to see the show," Owens replied.

"We?"

Owens pulled Dooley along as he stepped into the tent. "My name's Owens, and this here is my friend Dooley."

Dooley gave the chief a quick, nervous smile.

Chief Tall-Like-Oak stared at Owens for a long moment, and then he motioned for both boys to sit down on blankets nearby. "I have seen your people before," he told Owens.

Owens's eyes went wide. "My family?" he asked. "You've been to London before?"

"No," the chief replied. "I have seen your people in my land."

"He means people with your color," Dooley exclaimed.

Chief Tall-Like-Oak nodded. "Some work the land. Some wear blue coats and patrol our reservation."

"You mean some of them are soldiers?" Owens asked eagerly. "My father was a soldier. He died in a war."

"My son died in a war." Tall-Like-Oak smiled proudly. "He was a mighty warrior."

Dooley couldn't understand the Indian's broad smile. "Don't you miss him?"

Tall-Like-Oak's expression became solemn. "Yes," he replied in a deep voice. "But my people do not mourn the dead as you do. It is not a warrior's way to show fear, or pain . . . or sadness."

Owens and Dooley glanced at each other, feeling confused. Every story they'd heard about Indians told of wild, angry men. Even what they'd seen at the Wild West show the day before had painted the same picture.

Yet here the chief sat, legs crossed in front of him, hands resting on his knees, a man of quiet dignity.

Dooley wondered if the Indian was up to something. Would Tall-Like-Oak suddenly spring on them when they least expected it? Dooley eased toward the tent's opening just in case.

The chief seemed to sense the boy's fear and smiled again.

"Now you have met an Indian," Tall-Like-Oak said. "Is that why you came?"

"Er, no," Owens said, shaking off some of his own nervousness. "We're trying to help Buffalo Bill find out who attacked the copper, uh, I mean the police constable. The man in the blue uniform."

Chief Tall-Like-Oak's eyes narrowed, and Dooley felt a renewed urge to dash out of the tent. "Silent Eagle did not attack the blue coat," the chief said angrily. "He did not attack the other one either. I have never even heard of him."

"You mean Mr. Pryke?"

Tall-Like-Oak nodded. He stood up and suddenly seemed far more powerful, despite his age.

"We should be going now." Dooley's voice quavered as he turned toward the opening. "Come along, Owens."

Owens was tempted to rush from the tent too, but his desire for information wouldn't let him. "How can you be sure?" he asked.

"Why do you help Pahaska?"

"Who?" Owens asked.

"Pahaska," Tall-Like-Oak replied. "That is the name we have given Cody."

"Oh," Dooley replied. "Colonel Cody is famous, and he's been nice to us. We want to help, and he said we could."

"Did Silent Eagle tell you he didn't do it?" Owens asked.

"Silent Eagle is proud and strong," the chief replied. "He has been this way ever since he was a boy."

"He's not very friendly," Dooley said nervously.

"When he was a boy," Tall-Like-Oak explained, "he saw his home destroyed. He saw his family forced to move onto a reservation. There was sickness and hunger. He spoke out against these things and was beaten. He fought back and was locked up in a jail."

"Cor," Dooley gasped. "We've always heard that you Indians attack—" Dooley stopped short as he met the Indian's steady gaze.

"There is more to our story than your people will ever know," Tall-Like-Oak replied.

"Please tell us more about Silent Eagle," Owens said.

"He has always listened to the wisest of our people to understand our ways. Now he travels with Pahaska to learn more of the world of the white men."

Tall-Like-Oak stepped outside the tent, and the two boys followed him. "Silent Eagle fights only when he has to," the chief told them. "He sees much but speaks only when there is something he must say. That is how he was named. He is a Sioux warrior and would not attack an unarmed man."

"It sure doesn't sound like he would," Owens said. "But somebody took a gun to the constable and then *scalped* him. Do you have any idea who?"

Tall-Like-Oak shook his head. "I have seen that blue-coat soldier guarding the way into the camp," he told the boys. "He showed great bravery facing the buffalo with Silent Eagle."

Both Owens and Dooley froze as the importance of Tall-Like-Oak's words became clear in their minds.

"You mean the copper, I mean constable, who was attacked was the same one who helped stop the buffalo the other day?" Dooley asked the Indian chief.

Tall-Like-Oak nodded.

Owens knew that he and Dooley were thinking the same thing. Maybe the Indian was guilty after all. The constable was the same one who had teased the Indian the day the buffalo escaped. Everyone there had seen Silent Eagle's anger at the bantering. This gave the police a motive for the attack.

They'd have the one thing they needed to prove his guilt—and get him hanged.

Chapter 9

THEY HAD TO WAIT A LITTLE BIT TO GET INTO THE Wild West show site, but Wiggins and Jennie finally caught up with Owens and Dooley. Wiggins decided to spend some of the money Buffalo Bill gave them on train tickets back to Mile End Road. There was so much to talk about, he barely noticed the disapproving glances from the other passengers. Poor lads and lasses from the East End didn't normally ride London's Underground trains.

The discussion continued in their familiar meeting place in the back room of the Raven Pub.

"All right, what do we know?" Wiggins sighed, plopping down onto a stool. "The coppers can build a case against Silent Eagle. Constable Turnbuckle made a remark that Silent Eagle took the wrong way. So Silent Eagle beat him and scalped him. After J. Montague Pryke started making noise in Parliament and in the newspapers, Silent Eagle went after him too."

Dooley's eyes were wide with dismay. Owens gave a stiff nod, but Jennie shook her head. "How did Silent Eagle learn that it was Pryke he should go after?"

"Exactly," Wiggins agreed. "I don't imagine those Indians sitting down with the morning newspaper."

"Someone could have mentioned the story to them," Owens pointed out.

"Or read it to them," Jennie added.

"That's true," Dooley agreed.

"Then there's the big clue that led the police to Silent Eagle," Wiggins continued. "The porcupine quill with purple beads. That came from his costume in the show. But I can't imagine him wearing it while he attacked Pryke."

"No." Jennie frowned. "You're right. At first glance, things might hold together, but they really don't make sense. If we can see the problems, a good lawyer could tear this case to pieces in a courtroom."

"And you can bet Buffalo Bill would hire a good lawyer," Owens said.

"So Silent Eagle would get off—even if everyone was all angry?" Dooley asked.

"Someone certainly wanted people all stirred up," Wiggins said. "Angry enough, maybe, to kill Silent Eagle before he even faced a judge and jury."

"They're stirred up, all right," Dooley said. "While we visited with him, the chief told us that people are now booing the Indians' acts in the Wild West show."

"I heard someone turned up at the exposition grounds last night, throwing horse turds at the American eagle on the front of the building." Owens laughed. "I wouldn't want that job of cleaning *that* up. The coppers chased them off, or they'd have cut down the flag too."

"And you think someone's paid for all of this?" Jennie asked Wiggins.

"Why not?" Wiggins jumped up to pace around the room. "When we got involved in our first mystery, we stumbled on a group of posh folks aiming for high stakes. Maybe this is the same thing."

The door to the pub swung open, breaking his train of thought. Mr. Pilbeam, the owner of the Raven Pub, came in. It was a little hard to read his expression behind the impressive salt-and-pepper whiskers that curled from his sideburns to meet across his upper lip.

"I thought I heard you come in," the pub owner said. "Benny Flagg has been in here having a few pints and telling everyone about his adventures out in Earl's Court." He glanced over at Wiggins. "He talked a bit about your adventures too."

"We didn't do anything wrong," Dooley said anxiously.

"I didn't say you did," Pilbeam replied. "We just got word that Benny's horse turned up at his stable. Whoever stole the poor beast probably treated him better than Benny did. There was a poultice of grass and leaves over the sore spot on his shoulder."

Cries for more drinks came from the pub, and Pilbeam went back to the outer room. Wiggins and his friends looked at one another.

Jennie asked the obvious question. "Where would Silent Eagle find grass and leaves around here?"

Owens frowned. "Someone's garden, maybe?"

"Sure," Wiggins said sarcastically. "Most people would never notice an Indian climbing over their garden wall to borrow a few fixings for a stolen horse."

"There's Victoria Park," Dooley suggested. "My da takes me there sometimes on a Sunday."

"That's a good three-quarters of a mile away," Jennie said. "And the place is awfully public."

"So, we need a place with green things that's close, not too public, where people wouldn't notice someone digging." Wiggins frowned, then looked up. "The Tower Hamlets Cemetery."

"A churchyard?" Jennie said in surprise.

"It's bigger than that," Wiggins replied. "There's a wall around the place so people can't see in. The graveyard is also near the gasworks—not so many people round about there."

He got up and headed for the door. "Maybe we should go and take a look before the coppers hear about this and come searching."

Less than ten minutes of walking brought them within sight of the brick walls surrounding the cemetery. Wiggins began dragging his feet. "My little brother is buried here," he said. "It's where they put people who are too poor to pay for a funeral—thousands and thousands of them, I was told."

He shook his head, forcing the tears away.

"There might be someone at the gates," he said, his voice gruff.

Jennie eyed the bricks. "I bet we could climb that wall."

They all did, although Dooley needed a boost. Wiggins looked around at the cramped rows of crosses and statues that rose all around him. This was the private part of the cemetery, where people could buy plots. There were even a few aboveground mausoleums. The tombs were older. Almost fifty years of weather and London's smoky, cindery air had left all the stonework looking dingy.

His heart sank. The place was a quarter-mile square. How could they hope to find Silent Eagle if he didn't want to be found?

Jennie stepped forward. "Excuse me, Mr. Silent Eagle," she said, not shouting but in a very clear voice. "I'm hoping you may remember us. We're friends of Colonel Cody—" She glanced back at her friends. "What did Chief Tall-Like-Oak call him?"

"Pahaska," Owens told her.

"We're friends of Pahaska," she went on. "You saw us at his tent the other day. And we saw you today when the police came for you."

"I tried to help you," Wiggins added, "with the keys."

"And we want to help you now," Jennie added.

Wiggins wasn't sure where the man came from. One moment, all he saw was stonework; the next moment, Silent Eagle stood in front of them. Dooley took a half step back and behind Wiggins.

The warrior gazed at them for a long moment, then nodded. "Silent Eagle remembers." He gave them a half smile. "I do not think the blue-coat soldiers would send such young ones as trackers. So I will believe—and hope—you come to help me."

"We don't think you done—did—nothing." Dooley spoke up. Still, he remained hidden behind the others.

"I did not hurt the blue-coat man," Silent Eagle said. "He made me angry because I believed he mocked me when the buffalo got loose. But Pahaska explained to me that the man thought we should laugh together after facing danger, so I did not stay angry."

"We saw what you did with the buffalo," Owens said. "You were brave, and your quick thinking saved a lot of people. Not like that bloke with no chin."

Nodding, Silent Eagle lightly struck his own chin with the side of his hand, as if he were cutting it off. "That one did not know what to do. Zeke Black brought him from the big boat. Two of our buffalo had died, so they brought some more across the Great Water. Only one survived the journey, though. Zeke Black brought it to the camp, along with that useless man. I tried to explain this to the little man who does business for Pahaska."

"Mr. Salsbury?" Owens asked.

Silent Eagle scowled. "I do not trust that one. He walked away, and I decided to go to Pahaska. But the blue coats would not let me out."

"So you climbed over the wall," Wiggins said.

The Indian nodded, looking surprised. "But when I came to Pahaska's house, that one—Salsbury—was already there. I returned to the camp. Then the blue coats came to take me, saying I almost killed a man, a chief who counsels Grandmother England."

Dooley poked his head around Wiggins. "Who?"

"I think he means the queen," Jennie said.

Silent Eagle nodded. "The old woman who came to us in a great shining wagon. Many came with her, but I did not see this chief. I do not know him. How then could I fight with him?"

The Indian looked down at his hands. "Since I went to the reservation, I have not carried a weapon, except for the ones they give me when we ride for the people. And those can do no harm."

He glanced at his young listeners. "When a red man goes out among the white men in strange places, it is not good to have a knife or gun."

"I guess not," Wiggins said.

"Pahaska asked me to travel with him, and I agreed so I might learn the white man's secrets." Silent Eagle smiled bitterly. "I went to learn how they could defeat my people so many times. Then I saw how you live— so many pressed together, so many greedy people, so much lying."

He shook his head. "And when they come to punish those who do evil, you lock them behind stone walls."

"What do you do?" Jennie asked.

"We drive them out or we kill them."

Wiggins couldn't control the sudden chill that ran through his body. Indians lived a very different life from the folk of London town—even the poorest— with much harsher rules. Yet he absolutely believed that Silent Eagle was innocent.

The Indian's voice was matter-of-fact as he continued. "Better for a red man to lie as one of those buried here, behind stone walls, than to live that way. I thought these things while I stayed here, after I sent the horse on its way. For I realized I was alone in Grandmother England's land, where many white men and great waters stood between me and the plains that are my home. Then I said to myself, 'I will sing my death song, go out of this place, and die fighting.'"

"But you're not alone," Owens said. "We believe you."

"I am glad for that," the Indian replied. "But there are many powerful men who do not believe me."

"If you die, people will *never* believe you and the one who really did the evil won't be found," Jennie explained. "Colonel Cody—Pahaska—will help fight to clear your name. You must find a place to stay safe until he can help you."

"And where would that be?" Wiggins asked. "The coppers will be round here soon enough. Even if we had room for a boarder, I don't think my mam would jump at the idea."

"Nor mine," Owens had to admit.

"I can't see getting him up the stairs in our place," Dooley said. "Too many people about."

"Mr. Pilbeam?" Jennie suggested.

Wiggins shook his head. "He was a yeoman of the guard, protecting the queen. I don't see him hiding someone on the run from the law." The pub owner was sweet on Wiggins's mother and had done many favors for the family. But this would be one favor too many. "Besides," Wiggins went on, "there are too many sets of eyes around the Raven."

"Maybe—" Owens drew the word out, his voice tentative.

"Maybe what?" Jennie asked.

"Or who?" Wiggins said.

"Mr. Shears," Owens said. "He doesn't like Pryke, and he was suspicious about this whole hooraw. If we explain everything to him, he might be willing to help—at least for a little while."

Skulking through the back alleys, they came to Mr. Shears's barbershop quickly enough. Owens and the members of the Raven League had a longer time convincing Mr. Shears to help Silent Eagle.

At last, Shears agreed. "There's a deal of clutter in back," he warned. "It's closer to a storage closet than a room."

"As long as there's space for Silent Eagle to sit." Jennie glanced nervously at the Indian warrior. "You won't mind, will you?"

Silent Eagle shrugged. "Better here than in the white man's jail."

"Just one thing." Shears glanced at the razors and scissors neatly lined up along the counter. "Any cutting of hair around here, I do it."

Even Silent Eagle smiled at that.

"We'll bring you some food," Jennie promised, "and a change of clothes. I have a friend at a tailor's shop. They'll give me some old clothes."

"Will you go back to Pahaska's camp?" Silent Eagle asked. "I must send messages to him and Tall-Like-Oak."

"We'll bring them tomorrow." Jennie scribbled notes as Silent Eagle spoke.

While they worked, Wiggins frowned, a thought coming to him. "If Mr. Holmes had been handling this case, the first thing he'd have done was to examine the scene of the crime," he said. "That's what we'll do—first thing in the morning."

Chapter  10

"THIS IS BETTER THAN HANGING FROM THE BACK OF some wagon." Dooley eagerly leaned forward into the wind.

"So long as you don't tumble off the front." Jennie caught hold of Dooley's belt, pulling him back. She sat in front with Dooley, trying to look calm and collected.

"You act like this is your first time on an omnibus," Owens teased.

"It is," Dooley admitted cheerfully. "And I bet you've never been on one neither."

"Face it, carrottop," Owens shot back from the seat across, where he sat with Wiggins. "None of us have ever been on one of these."

Wiggins chuckled. "True." The omnibus was a double-decker affair with seats inside and on the roof. A single flight of narrow stairs curled up the back end of the horse-drawn public transport to the top—which was where he and his friends had decided to sit on their journey back out to the Wild West encampment. When they met this morning, the bus had been Wiggins's first choice.

"Wouldn't the Underground have been faster?" Owens asked. They'd had to change buses several times since they set off on the journey.

"Sure," Wiggins replied sarcastically. "And it would have eaten up the money Colonel Cody gave us a lot quicker too."

They arrived at the show grounds and quickly headed for the second footbridge—the one that led to the corral.

"All right," Wiggins said, stopping next to the stables that flanked the entrance to the bridge. "This is where the constable was attacked. So any clues left behind will be right around here."

"You mean if there are any clues," Dooley corrected.

Wiggins tried to adopt a stern expression. "No, I don't," he replied. "Mr. Holmes says there are always clues; you just have to look for them the right way. . . ." He struggled for a moment, trying to remember the right words. "Don't simply see, *observe*."

"We also have to get these messages to Colonel Cody and to Chief Tall-Like-Oak," reminded Owens.

"There aren't too many people around here now," Jennie pointed out, "but that might change."

Wiggins thought for a moment, then grinned. "All right, then," he replied. "You and Dooley start looking. Owens and I will join you after we deliver the messages."

"But I want to—"

"Grand!" Owens called back as he and Wiggins ran off. "We'll be back soon."

Dooley gave Jennie a look. "Well, isn't this nice? They go off and leave us to muck around. I think Wiggins just put us together 'cause he thinks I need a minder."

"Perhaps he just thinks we work well together," Jennie said. "Remember our first case?"

Dooley immediately brightened. "Maybe you're right." He quickened his step. "Well, then let's get to it."

For several minutes, Jennie and Dooley wandered about the entrance to the bridge, looking at the ground. They made wider and wider circles, then started looking inside the stables. The painstaking search quickly left Dooley feeling frustrated, especially since he wasn't really sure what they were looking for.

"This isn't getting us anywhere," he complained.

Jennie was peeking over the rail into one of the empty horse stalls. "You have to be more patient," she advised. "If it was easy to find, the police would already have it."

"You don't know some of our coppers," Dooley muttered, kicking a wisp of hay.

After a few more minutes, Dooley drifted out onto the footbridge. He leaned against the railing and looked down onto the tracks below. *Maybe a train will come by,* he thought, *and cover the whole bridge in a cloud of steam. Would that be like flying in a cloud?*

His daydream stopped when he caught a glimpse of yellow and white on the embankment just behind the stable. The ground that sloped down to the tracks was covered with small stones and gravel. A spindly bush had managed to push its way to sunlight. Whatever it was—a book or magazine—had caught under a branch.

Dooley could see it was beyond his reach. Maybe he could climb over and grab it. But someone might see him, or, worse yet, he might roll down the steep hillside right into the path of an oncoming train. Then he remembered the pitchfork leaning against one of the stable stalls.

In a flash, Dooley grabbed the tool and returned to the bridge. Jennie never noticed him as she poked around for clues three stalls down.

Leaning as far as he could, Dooley reached out with the pitchfork. Holding it by the very end of the handle, he eased one of the fork's prongs between the pages. The magazine folded over the prong as Dooley slowly lifted up the tool and pulled it back toward him.

Just as he brought the pitchfork over the stone wall of the bridge, the magazine started to slip off the prong. Dooley quickly yanked back with one hand and reached over the railing with the other to grab the publication just as it fell.

It was in fairly good condition, medium-sized with a softbound yellow cover. Dooley couldn't read the title or any of the other words on the cover or inside, but a picture caught his eye.

The illustration on the front showed British constables capturing a hard-looking ruffian. A quick glimpse at the first few pages revealed similar illustrations of criminal types and police officers.

Suddenly, he heard Jennie let out a small, sharp cry. Tucking the magazine inside his shirt, he snatched up the pitchfork and ran into the stable. He found Jennie in a stall, backing away from a rough-looking man in a checked shirt as he demanded, "What are you doing here?"

Dooley immediately recognized Zeke Black, the roustabout who had caught them sneaking into the show. "Get away from her!" he cried, charging forward.

Zeke batted the prongs away from his body, then grabbed the pole. Dooley tried to hold on in spite of being flung about. The pitchfork twisted out of his hands as he stumbled back into Jennie. Zeke had spun him around. Now they were both trapped in the stall. The big man loomed over them, pitchfork in hand. "What are *both* of you brats doing back here?"

"We're just looking around," Jennie tried to explain. "We've never seen anything like this before—"

"Seems you're always looking around and asking questions," Zeke growled. "Funny thing happens to nosy people. They usually get their noses broken."

Before Zeke could take another step, a voice rang out behind him.

"There they are!"

Dooley let out a long breath when Wiggins and Owens walked up to the stall. It was even better to see Colonel Cody and Chief Tall-Like-Oak behind them.

"We keep running into you," Wiggins said, stepping between Jennie and Zeke. "Funny, ain't it?"

"Is there a problem here, Zeke?" Cody asked his employee.

"Every time I turn around, I catch these kids sneaking round the place," Zeke growled.

"They're running errands for me now, so they can come and go as they please," Colonel Cody said.

Zeke stared hard at Wiggins. "Odd how bad things seem to happen when they're around—that copper nearly gets killed, Silent Eagle gets arrested, then that man Pryke—"

"We didn't do none of those things," Dooley shouted. "In fact, we're trying—"

"To stay out of trouble," Wiggins interrupted. "That's why we're running errands and things for folks like Colonel Cody here." He gave Dooley a sharp look.

Dooley stared for a moment, then realized why Wiggins had cut him off. It wouldn't do for too many people to know what they were up to.

"It's all right, Zeke," Cody told the cowboy. "I know we're all a little jumpy right now, but these kids are fine. Why don't you go make sure our people are on the job? I think keeping busy is the best thing for us all."

"Sure," Zeke said dryly. He turned and walked off toward the main arena.

Owens shuddered as the cowhand walked away. "He really doesn't like us," he told the others.

"Many Western folk are hard men," Cody explained. "Have to be to live out in the wilderness. If you have no family and you're far from home, well . . ."

Dooley snorted in Zeke's direction. "You're far from America, but you're not grumpy."

Cody smiled. "Zeke's even farther from his home," he said. "He's from a part of Canada, way up north."

"Did you give Colonel Cody and Chief Tall-Like-Oak the messages from Silent Eagle?" Jennie asked.

"Yes, little missy." Cody spoke up. "We're both glad that he's safe . . . for now." He shook his head. "Though we're not happy that you children are in the middle of this. I've seen lynch mobs before. They're an ugly sight."

"The face of hate is always ugly," the chief added glumly.

"I'd like to ask something," Jennie said. "Why don't Silent Eagle and Mr. Salsbury get along?"

Buffalo Bill shook his head. "It was something that happened on the voyage over. Remember, none of the Indians had ever been on the ocean. The water was rough, and when they got seasick—"

Chief Tall-Like-Oak groaned at the memory. "We began singing our death songs."

"Nate saved the day," Cody went on. "Before being a manager, he was an actor. He recited pieces, sang, and danced—most of the Indians loved him for cheering them up."

The chief frowned. "But to Silent Eagle, Salsbury seemed to have two faces. He would not trust him."

"And when Nate saw how Silent Eagle was treating him, well, things just went downhill."

"I see," Jennie said.

Wiggins glanced around to see if anyone was nearby. "Colonel Cody will help us hide Silent Eagle," he told Jennie and Dooley quietly.

"Just until I can get some friends here to guarantee his safety when he turns himself in," Cody explained.

"He won't do that," Owens told the colonel. "He said he'd rather die than rot in jail."

"And Dartmoor Prison is a far cry from the open—whatdeyecallit—range," Dooley added.

"It's not safe for him on the run." Cody's voice was firm. "It's not safe for you either. Especially since you've told me that Sherlock Holmes is away."

"We have to help Silent Eagle prove his innocence," Wiggins insisted. "We promised."

He glanced around at the faces of his friends. Despite their differences, each one held the same determined expression.

Buffalo Bill must have seen their commitment too. "You've got it in your minds to do this no matter what I say, don't you?"

Before any of them could answer, Chief Tall-Like-Oak placed a hand on Owens's shoulder. "They gave their word," he said. "That still means much to them."

Cody bowed his head for a moment. "Very well," he said finally. "But it means that I'm going to be more involved in this too. Just as soon as I get some of the local bigwigs to take a real look at this case."

The Raven Leaguers cheered in unison.

"There's one way you can help right now," Wiggins told the frontiersman. "In the hospital, Constable Turnbuckle mumbled something about smuggling."

Cody frowned. "Smuggling what?"

"He didn't say," Jennie replied.

"Could it be buffalos?" Owens suggested.

Cody removed his Stetson and scratched his head. "Not likely," he said. "Most everyone in the show is a Westerner, born or raised. They might know about cattle rustling—"

"Well, that's an animal," Owens pointed out.

"Yes," Cody agreed, "but rustling cattle is different from smuggling. Some rustlers might run them across the border into Mexico—but they wouldn't have the contacts to move things across the Atlantic Ocean."

"Oh," Dooley muttered.

"Smugglers would need connections with ships' captains and crews, merchants in ports, maybe dockworkers," Cody said. "Besides, there are no laws saying you can't move buffalo from place to place, so there's no profit in doing it secretly, if you see what I mean."

"Mr. Holmes would have thought of that," Wiggins mumbled. "Why didn't I?"

"You're doing fine," Cody told Wiggins. "You all are. Now the chief and I have to go meet with some folks." Cody reached into his pocket, pulling out a handful of coins, and gave them to Wiggins. "Please buy Silent Eagle whatever he needs and let me know if you need more."

"All right, Colonel Cody," Wiggins called out as the frontiersman and Tall-Like-Oak walked away. "And we'll meet back with you tomorrow." He stared after the pair of Westerners. "I can't help feeling that we just heard something—"

"Well, what he said didn't help us with the smuggling clue," Dooley complained.

Wiggins snapped his fingers. "Maybe it did," he said. "Maybe it did."

Chapter 11

THE RAVEN LEAGUE WAS JUST LEAVING THE performers' encampment when Wiggins spotted a familiar figure approaching them from the opposite end of the bridge. Inspector Desmond wasn't his usual elegant self. The detective's suit was wrinkled and saggy at the knees, he hadn't shaved, and Wiggins spotted telltale bags under the man's eyes. Desmond had obviously been up all night searching for Silent Eagle. Lack of sleep and lack of success hadn't improved his temper.

"What are you lot doing here?" he demanded when he saw them. "Snooping, were you? Has Sherlock Holmes decided to push his long nose into this business?"

Wiggins was about to respond just as sharply when he bit back his words. *It won't help things to get this copper angry at us,* he thought. So how could he answer? "Maybe we are," he said. "Or maybe we're earning a few bob running errands for Colonel Cody." He fumbled in his pocket. "See? He wrote up a special pass for us and all."

Desmond examined the card Wiggins held out, glared at Wiggins and the others, and finally shook his head and smiled. "I suppose I should admire such an industrious attitude—whoever you may be working for."

Several uniformed constables had drifted over, looking to their superior for a clue on how to treat the youngsters. Inspector Desmond waved them away. "Off with you now," he said to Wiggins and the Raven Leaguers. "I have some business with Colonel Cody myself."

Wiggins and the others didn't need a second invitation. Walking away from the exhibition grounds, Wiggins took a moment to look back, just to make sure Inspector Desmond wasn't peering after them. He wasn't, so Wiggins led the way to the Underground station, deciding to spend some of Colonel Cody's money on a train ride home.

They wound up with a compartment all to themselves. Wiggins slumped in his seat. "This is getting as complicated as our last case."

Owens nodded. "And this time, we don't have Sherlock Holmes to help us sort things out."

Dooley ran his fingers through his tousled hair. "I don't know how he can remember everything to do with a mystery."

"I know what you mean," Wiggins admitted. "All the time we were talking with Buffalo Bill, I kept worrying that I had forgotten things I ought to be asking about."

"Maybe Sherlock Holmes can hold everything in his head, but we don't have to." Jennie drew her notebook and pencil from a pocket. "Let's write down everything we know, then we can come up with a list of things we don't know."

She licked the pencil lead and got ready to write.

Wiggins felt his lips twist into a wry grin. Jennie didn't have to say anything, but she might as well have taken that pencil and underlined how important it was for all of them to read and write.

"We know that the copper was nearly beaten to death and then scalped," Dooley began.

"But we don't know what he was doing around the stables that night," Owens pointed out. "He wasn't on duty. In fact, he wasn't even in uniform."

"And he wasn't actually shot. The newspapers got that wrong. Buffalo Bill's pistol was loaded with blanks. Turnbuckle wound up with powder burns and was beaten." Wiggins frowned. "I don't think it's likely he just happened to walk past the stables and spot a burglar coming out with Cody's gun."

"If it wasn't a burglar, then the attacker had to be connected with the show," Jennie said. "Perhaps there's another connection. Chief Tall-Like-Oak mentioned that Constable Turnbuckle was the one who stood up to that buffalo when it went wild."

"We know." Owens nodded. "Turnbuckle passed a remark that Silent Eagle didn't understand—and didn't like."

"But there were two other men involved in all that," Dooley said. "What about that big bloke who keeps chasing us? He was one."

"Zeke Black." Wiggins remembered the name. "He sure doesn't like us nosing around."

"And then there was the funny-looking fellow with no chin," Owens chimed in.

"Does he work for Buffalo Bill's Wild West?" Jennie asked. "They've been here almost four months. But Silent Eagle said that fellow came from the ship that just arrived from America—the one that brought the buffalo. Zeke Black brought him."

"All right, so we have two men connected to the constable." Owens rubbed his chin thoughtfully. "Where do we go from here?"

"Let's just suppose that Zeke Black is the attacker," Wiggins said. "Working backstage, it would have been easy enough for him to get hold of Buffalo Bill's gun. He could have been around the stables that evening."

Wiggins leaned back in his seat. "When Mr. Holmes investigates a crime, he looks for certain things, like the means of committing the crime and how the guilty person had the chance to commit it. We've just gone over those. Another thing Mr. Holmes looks for is the motive. *Why* would Zeke Black attack and scalp a copper?"

"Why would the chinless bloke do it?" Dooley asked in frustration.

"Scalping would set people looking in the wrong direction," Jennie replied. "Everyone would blame the attack on an Indian."

"And there are nearly a hundred of them at the Wild West camp," Wiggins said.

"But why would Zeke Black go after Mr. Pryke?" Dooley asked.

Wiggins raised a hand. "First things first. Why would Zeke Black use the gun on the copper?"

"A gun with blanks," Owens added. "He'd know that—he's part of the show."

Jennie looked up from her scribbling. "When Inspector Desmond tried to speak to Turnbuckle at the hospital, all he managed to say was 'smuggling' and 'buffalo.'"

"'Smuggling,'" Owens repeated, "and Zeke Black brought the buffalo from a ship that had just come from America."

"Maybe that ship brought more than buffalos," Wiggins muttered.

"Well, we know it brought the chinless man too," Jennie said. "Perhaps he was the buffalo's minder."

"That gink didn't know nothing about how to handle the beast." Dooley's voice was scornful.

"So his coming along wasn't much help," Wiggins said.

Owens laughed. "More like the opposite."

Wiggins nodded. "If Chinless had no experience with animals, why *did* Zeke bring him along?"

He snapped his fingers. "Remember what Buffalo Bill told us when we asked him about smuggling? He didn't think any of his people could be involved because they wouldn't have the connections with people on the ships."

Owens grinned. "But Zeke Black seems to have had a friend on this ship."

With a loud whoosh of steam, the train jerked to a halt. Jennie glanced out the window. "This is our stop!"

The train's conductor gave the members of the Raven League a dirty look as they barely managed to get off the train in time. They stood on the station platform, enveloped in clouds of steam and smoke.

"I hope you got all that written down," Dooley told Jennie.

"Oh, I don't think we'll be forgetting it very soon." Wiggins reached into his pocket. "Right now, though, we have a little business to take care of." He fished out half a crown and plopped the heavy coin into Jennie's hand. After a moment's thought, he added a few shillings more. "Will that be enough to feed Silent Eagle and get him a new set of clothes?"

She jingled the coins in her fist. "More than enough if I can get my friend Jacob to help."

Wiggins glanced at Owens. "Would you help too—with the carrying and such?"

Owens shot him a suspicious look. "And what will you be doing all the while?"

"Dooley and I will be visiting the docks," Wiggins replied. "Most everything that comes into London—legal and illegal—has to pass through there. The folks that work in the area have to see things."

He smiled at Dooley. "We need to learn about smuggling, and I'm hoping that some friend or other of your father's will have something to teach us."

Chapter 12

WIGGINS TOOK A DEEP BREATH, RELISHING THE BRACKISH smell in the air. He and Dooley had spent hours walking the docks, but Wiggins never tired of coming down here. On the few cases for Mr. Holmes that involved the river, he'd run into some truly amazing characters. Even the villains and scoundrels were more colorful than the common thugs of London's underworld.

There were men from many countries—India, Africa, even the South Sea Islands. And there was the booty—ivory, gold, even lost treasures of precious jewels.

Now it appeared that this case, even though it started with an Indian from America, was leading in the same direction. Down to the sea.

Well, at least down to the river, Wiggins corrected himself. He wondered if his friend shared his feelings about the docklands, especially since Dooley's father worked on land and sea as a carpenter and laborer. Certainly Dooley knew a lot of the dockworkers and sailors, and the boys had spent some time talking to many of them.

"So far we haven't learned much." Dooley sighed as they moved along the wharves. The cargo boats here seemed large enough to an ignorant landsman's eye, but Wiggins knew far-larger vessels pulled into the gigantic dockyards to load or unload cargo, while even larger oceangoing ships often put in farther downriver, closer to the sea.

"Most of the workers we spoke to wouldn't even talk to us once we mentioned smuggling." Wiggins poked Dooley with an elbow. "I hope that means they're honest men."

Dooley pulled his jacket closer, shivering. "I was thinking the same thing. What if word gets back to the people we're looking for?"

"That's why we're only talking to friends of your father," Wiggins replied, "and why I made up that story we're telling them. So don't give up. Now, who's next?"

Dooley pointed toward a teetering wreck of a flophouse held up, it seemed, only by the wisps of incoming fog. "That's where Old Crowe lives."

"Who?"

"Old Barnabas Crowe," Dooley replied. "He's been a sailor since before my father was even born."

Dooley squinted again as a short, dark figure exited the run-down building. "There he is! Come on!"

The two boys easily caught up with the old seaman, who seemed in no hurry to go anywhere in particular.

"Why, it's young William O'Dare," Barnabas Crowe declared cheerfully. "'Ow are ye, lad?"

Dooley grinned and shook his head. "I'm fine, and it's Doolan, sir—Dooley to my friends. You know my da. He works on—"

"Half the rigs on these docks," the old man finished for him. "Course I know him. What old salt worth his cast wouldn't?" He seemed to notice Wiggins for the first time. "Who be ye, boy?"

"This is Wiggins," Dooley answered eagerly. "He's my friend, and—"

"I was about your age when I went to sea," Crowe told Wiggins. "That was on the old *Venture*. Grand ship out of . . ." He scratched his head. "Now, what was that port?"

"Sounds like a great story, sir," Wiggins said politely. "We've been trying to find out something very important, and Dooley thought you might have the answers."

"If it has anything to do with the sea, I'm your man." The old seaman took a seat on a nearby crate and motioned for the boys to do the same. "What's your question?"

Wiggins took a second to recall the details of his prepared story. "A friend of ours is in trouble," he explained. "He found some goods that didn't belong to him—"

"Stole 'em?" The old seaman scowled. "Got no time to palaver with a thief."

"No, sir," Dooley quickly declared. "He didn't steal nothing, and neither did we!"

"That's right," Wiggins added. "We think the, uh, things he found were brought here by smugglers. And if we don't find out who they are, our friend could wind up in trouble with the law."

"Smugglers, eh?" Barnabas Crowe rubbed his stubbled chin. "Now, there's a scurvy lot, to be sure."

Wiggins and Dooley leaned forward eagerly.

"They run about every port in the world the way rats swarm through the sewers," Crowe told them.

"They'll steal anything, lie through their teeth, and slit your throat for a tumbler of gin and a song."

Dooley shuddered and then glanced around the almost-empty street. Wiggins tried to appear as if this were old news to him, but he felt almost as uneasy as his friend.

"Seen 'em in every port I traveled," the old seaman went on.

"Even here in London?" Wiggins asked.

"Oh, aye," Old Crowe replied. "More here than in most places. That's because London is a rich port city."

Crowe fumbled in his old peacoat to pull out a stained clay pipe. "Even with open trade, there still be bounty that folks want, but the law says otherwise."

"Like what?" Dooley asked. All around, the evening fog began to roll in. The buzz of a busy and crowded seaport slowly faded, replaced by the sound of lapping waves and a calm but eerie quiet.

"Folks might want to bring goods in without giving the queen her due."

Seeing the puzzled expression on Dooley's face, he explained, "They don't want to pay no duty, uh, taxes, on tea, tobacco, and suchlike. If they get caught, it's off to prison, and their goods are burned here on the docks." He frowned as he lit his pipe. "Burnin' good tobacco. You'd think they could give it away free."

"Is that all they smuggle?" Wiggins asked.

Old Crowe laughed. "No, no, lad. All sorts of things come through. Opium, I hear—and even people."

"People!" Dooley exclaimed.

"I hear tales." The seaman blew smoke from between his yellow teeth. "How do you think all the Chinese folk are turning up in Limehouse?"

Wiggins knew some of the old tales of brandy and wine being smuggled in from the Continent, but this sounded much bigger. "How can they get away with it?" he asked in amazement. "The police must know what you know."

"Ha!" The sarcasm in Crowe's voice was thick. "Nay, laddie, they know some of what I know. But ye have to realize that the smugglers have been at this longer than there's been a law."

The old sailor closed his eyes thoughtfully. "Some of those gangs go back three or four generations," he said. "Their course is sure and their channels clear."

Crowe opened his eyes and must have noticed the boys' confusion. "I mean, they have all their connections set, all the right people in place."

Both boys nodded. Colonel Cody had told them much the same thing earlier.

"There's captains, crews, and port officials to be paid off," Crowe went on. "Then, once you've got your cargo past them—and the honest lawmen—you need a place to hold your goods till your . . . customers come for them."

"Sounds like a lot of business to take care of," Wiggins commented.

"I told you, lad." Crowe relit his pipe and took a few short puffs. "Some of the best smugglers been at this a long time. In fact, many fine old merchant families made their fortunes from smuggling rum, spices, and slaves."

"Old families?" Wiggins mused aloud.

"You mean some of the posh folks was criminals?" Dooley gasped.

"Still are." Crowe snorted. "Along with the folks they put in office."

Now Wiggins rubbed his chin thoughtfully. Could Pryke be involved in smuggling? Mr. Shears said he used to have a shabby little office, but now he was moving up the ladder of importance.

Maybe he was involved in smuggling, and some of his cronies turned on him—beat him up, Wiggins pondered. *Maybe Zeke was one of those cronies. If so, what were they smuggling?*

"Aye, they're a wild bunch of gentry, they are," Crowe added, speaking more to himself than the boys. "And to hear them talk, nobody can outsail, outfight, or outdrink 'em. But I showed 'em. Showed 'em up good." A leer appeared on the old man's craggy face. "I can 'andle me drink and me fists."

"You had to fight 'em?" Wiggins asked, trying not to seem too eager. "Where?"

"Quite a few places," Old Crowe admitted. "Never too far from pier or port. Smugglers, they like being close to water in case they have to leave sudden-like."

"But where in London?" Wiggins pressed.

"Oh, pubs like the Oak and Ivy, the Midnight Flit, the Bucket. Dangerous places, they be. Best keep your teeth in your head, your back to the wall, and your coin out of sight."

"We will," Dooley assured him.

"Eh?" Crowe blinked, jarred out of his memories.

"Nothing, sir," Wiggins said, grabbing Dooley by the arm. "He was just caught up in your story."

Crowe eyed them suspiciously. "Don't you be goin' near them places, boys," he warned in earnest. "One wrong word or step and they'll find your bodies in the Thames."

The warning hit home for both boys. The memory of Dooley's brother, Tim, found floating in the river, was still fresh and painful.

"We're just getting information," Wiggins told the old sailor. "Like I said, to tell our friend."

"To be sure, that's all it better be," the old salt warned.

"Thanks for your help, sir," Dooley added.

"You're welcome, young Dorley."

"Dooley, sir. Dooley."

"Aye. I know that."

Wiggins and Dooley said their good-byes and left the old sailor still sitting on the crate, smoking his pipe.

The shadows were getting longer now, and the docks were almost deserted. The fog had become thicker, seeming to curl and slither along the damp wood of the pier.

"Well, that gave us a lot to tell the others," Wiggins said. "Especially that part about the rich folks and their connections."

"That's true," Dooley agreed. "But there's so much going on, so much to remember."

"Jennie will write it all down," Wiggins said. "That'll help. Let's hurry."

Eager to meet up with the others, Wiggins and Dooley raced along a particularly desolate part of the docks. During the day, it was jammed with workers, peddlers, and their customers. But now, they saw closed shops, stacked crates, and piles of garbage. The boys were used to the usual vermin that came with this area, but the wharf rats that suddenly stepped out of the shadows were the two-legged kind.

They were large, muscular men, with unshaven faces and worn, ill-fitting clothes. One was bald with a scar that ran down the length of his right cheek. The other had dark, greasy hair. Even from eight feet away, Wiggins and Dooley could tell neither had seen a bath in some time.

"Well, lookee what we have here," Baldy said, gesturing toward the boys. For the first time, Wiggins saw that he had a knife in that hand. "A bit late for two young tykes to be about these parts."

"Dangerous parts, at that." The other man sneered.

"If that's so," Wiggins said as he and Dooley backed away, "we'll just be on our way."

They quickly turned, then stopped as a third ruffian appeared beside a stack of crates behind them. He was tall and thin, his skin burned dark by the sun. This time Wiggins immediately saw the item in his hand, a small wooden club about twelve inches long. Sailors called them belaying pins. They had many uses on a ship, but here on land, Wiggins could think of only one purpose.

He grabbed Dooley and cut left, going up and over the stack of crates. As the thugs came around the obstacle, the boys jumped onto a pile of garbage, rolled out of it, and ran down a narrow alley between two old buildings.

Wiggins could hear the men shouting and footfalls thudding in pursuit. He and Dooley reached the end of the alley and turned down another narrow passage, hoping it would bring them out onto a busier street.

Dooley staggered into Wiggins as they reached the alley mouth, letting out a cry of dismay. They faced a wharf and warehouse in an area more isolated than anywhere they'd been before.

Forcing a final burst of speed out of his legs, Wiggins darted across the wharf, hoping to find a boat tied up there. No luck. Behind him, Dooley struggled with the doors to the warehouse—they were locked. The younger boy joined Wiggins, staring down at the water.

"Can't swim," Dooley whimpered in a tiny voice. They turned around just as the three men appeared at the landward end of the wharf.

"I don't like to run, brats," the greasy-haired one wheezed, struggling to catch his breath. "Makes me mad, like you made others mad with your snoopin'."

"That's enough," the tall, thin one said. "Let's just teach 'em and be on our way."

The three men came toward them. Old Crowe's warning echoed in Wiggins's mind: *They'll find your bodies in the Thames.* He curled up a trembling fist and saw Dooley do the same. But they both knew they had no chance against these thugs.

"I'm sorry, Dooley." Those were the only words Wiggins could think of as he saw the thin man raise the belaying pin.

"That will be enough of that!"

The shout came from somewhere behind the thugs. All three of them turned around as the voice called out again.

"Constable Garrett, throw your light on them!"

Though the fog was thicker here, the boys could see a lantern go on about ten feet back the way they had come.

"This is the police," the voice shouted from another position in the pea soup mist. This time Wiggins thought he recognized the commanding tones. "Put down your weapons and step forward."

"Jiggers, it's the law!" Baldy instantly slipped his knife into his belt. "Best get out of here!"

The three men pushed past the boys to the far end of the wharf, disappearing in the fog to the sound of three loud splashes.

"They jumped into the river!" Dooley called. "Come quick, you lot, or they'll get away!"

He blinked as only Inspector Desmond came out of the thick, greasy mist.

"Where are the other coppers, uh, policemen?" Dooley asked.

Desmond smiled. "This way." He walked them back off the wharf to where a barrel of tar sat against a wall. A bull's-eye lantern sat on top, its white light much brighter as they came close.

"You're alone," Dooley said in amazement.

"When you don't carry a weapon and the bad ones do," the inspector replied, "you have to keep your wits about you. That's what you boys need to be doing," Desmond told them. "Keep your wits about you, and keep your nose out of police business. These are dangerous people hereabouts."

"We know that," Dooley said.

"You know more than that, I think," Desmond continued. "If it's anything that can help with this case, you need to tell me . . . now."

Wiggins wanted to tell the officer about Silent Eagle's innocence. But to explain how he knew, Wiggins would have to mention talking with Silent Eagle—and where, giving away the Indian's hiding place. Besides, all they had were suspicions. As Mr. Holmes was always saying, deductions without facts were useless.

"We really don't have anything to tell you, Inspector," Wiggins said finally. "But believe me, we'll get on to you the moment we know something. Honest."

"Pardon?" Desmond raised an inquisitive eyebrow.

"*If* we find something out, sir," Wiggins said. He cleared his throat, then began pushing Dooley along ahead of him. "Well, thanks for saving us. We'll be seeing you!"

"I sincerely hope not," the police inspector called after them.

"You should have seen them run!" Dooley stood on top of a keg in back of the Raven Pub. Wiggins, Jennie, and Owens were seated around the room, listening as he finished his tale about the attack on the wharf.

"It was amazing how Inspector Desmond tricked those villains," he said.

Jennie smiled. "Sounds like you're changing your mind about policemen."

"Nah," Dooley said. "Just him."

"We've all had a busy time of it," Owens said. "I took some food over to Silent Eagle, and Jennie bought him some clothes from that tailor friend's shop."

"Grand," Wiggins replied. "Now, if we could just figure out how everything we learned today fits together."

Jennie immediately dug out her little notebook. "Let's go over the notes I made," she suggested.

Wiggins and Owens leaned in, eager to hear her read back the facts they had collected. As Dooley bent forward, something crackled inside his shirt—the magazine he'd retrieved from behind the Wild West show stables. He had completely forgotten about it in all the excitement!

He crept back, sitting down in the dim space behind a barrel so he'd have the magazine to himself. Dooley dug it out and flipped through the pages. Many of them were covered with text, but here and there were pictures of hard-looking characters like the ones they'd seen on the docks. Dooley even recognized a face from the local newspapers—the posh jewel thief, Gentleman Jeremy Clive, being apprehended by detectives.

About halfway through the magazine, Dooley found several pages stuck together by a dark stain. Gingerly he separated each one, being careful not to tear them.

The last two came apart more easily, and Dooley was glad because there was a great picture on one. It showed what looked like a snake with a human face squirming out of a jail cell. Dooley chuckled and went to turn the page when something struck him.

That face looked familiar. Most of it was pretty unremarkable, but that bristly mustache and the way the jaw sloped back below his lips . . .

Dooley suddenly realized this was an exact likeness of the man they'd seen handling the buffalo the day Constable Turnbuckle had been shot. He jumped up.

"Look at this!" His excited cry turned into a yell of horror. Now that he was in the light, he could see that the sticky, reddish brown stuff that had glued the pages together was a large, unmistakable stain . . . dried blood!

Chapter 13

WIGGINS'S EYES MOVED QUICKLY FROM THE PICTURE ON the bloody page to Dooley's face. "Where did you get that?" he demanded.

"I found it, didn't I?" Dooley replied.

"Right," Wiggins said. "Where?"

"When you and Owens went and left us to muck around in the stables, I found it on the hill that goes down to the railway tracks—"

"The embankment," Jennie put in.

"Where all the stone and gravel is," Dooley went on. He explained how he'd rescued the magazine. "I was just putting away the pitchfork when Zeke Black turned up," he finished. "After the scare he gave us, I clean forgot I had this."

Jennie took the magazine and turned back to the soft yellow cover. *"The Policeman's World,"* she read, pointing to the title at the top of the page. "Under that it says, 'Illustrated news from around the globe for the Empire's law enforcers.'" She looked up. "Since it's in English, I expect they must mean the British Empire."

Owens nodded. "Americans wouldn't say that. I bet if you look inside, you'll see it's printed here in London."

Jennie riffled through the pages. "So, we have a British magazine full of international news and pictures, probably favored by a policeman—"

"Judging from all the blood on it, I think we can say it belonged to Constable Turnbuckle," Wiggins said. "And we can also say he had it when he was beaten."

"The same constable who was guarding the entrance when the buffalo began acting up," Jennie agreed. "He saw all three men involved and at some point made the connection between the chinless fellow and this picture in the magazine."

"The copper was out of uniform," Owens added. "So, he must have figured it out after he went home. He came right back to question the chinless man and was attacked."

"And scalped." Dooley shuddered.

"As Wiggins says, first things first," Jennie said. "When Constable Turnbuckle spoke to Inspector Desmond at the hospital, he said 'buffalo.' I think he was trying to say that one of the men with the buffalo attacked him. He also said 'smuggling.' That's the reason he was attacked."

"How do you get that?" Owens said in disbelief.

"What were they smuggling?" Dooley asked.

Jennie opened the magazine to the bloody page and pointed at the picture. "This story isn't about smuggling tobacco, jewels"—she glanced at Owens—"or buffalo. It's about smuggling people. Didn't that Old Crowe person mention that?"

"He talked about smuggling Chinese," Wiggins admitted.

"I think these people smuggle criminals." Jennie turned back to the page. "The print under the picture tells how a gangster called Chinless Ed Gorham made a getaway from jail in New York City. Now he's here in London."

At the word *getaway*, Wiggins suddenly turned to stare at Jennie.

"You want to argue?" she asked.

Slowly, he shook his head. "You made me remember something. A few times while we were working for Mr. Holmes, he sent out the Irregulars to get word of different villains he wanted to put his hands on. But it was like some of these blokes had vanished from London."

"Maybe they ended up dead," Owens said.

"Maybe." Wiggins shrugged. "But you know how you hear things round here—though you may not believe it all? Well, when a lot of these blokes vanished, I heard stories about a secret, special route for getaways. I wouldn't have called it smuggling, but when you put it that way. . . ."

"So what were these rumors about?" Jennie asked.

"The way I heard it," Wiggins said, "if London got too hot for business—"

"Thieving," Dooley said.

"If the coppers were really on your trail, you could get out of the city—even out of the country. It could cost a burglar everything he'd stolen, and even then, he might have to work off a debt wherever he wound up. Other kinds of villains could use the service too. Supposedly, some South American dictators have turned up in England—or gotten out— very quietly this way."

Owens raised his eyebrows. "Sounds like a pretty wild story to me."

Wiggins didn't offer any answer. But he could see everyone was thinking much the same thing. A month ago, they'd have thought a plot to assassinate the queen would be just as wild. Then they'd stumbled onto one.

"Maybe it's just thieves' gossip," Wiggins finally said. "But we have to dig into it tomorrow, and I can think of three places where we can try."

"Three?" said Dooley.

Wiggins nodded. "The pubs Old Crowe mentioned to us—the Oak and Ivy, the Midnight Flit, and the Bucket."

Dooley stared. "He also said we could get our throats cut."

"That's why we're not going to spy—we're going to work."

Jennie and Owens joined in the stare. "Doing what?" Owens demanded.

"Cleaning," Wiggins replied. "All of us did it for Mr. Pilbeam once at the Raven Pub."

The expressions on the other members of the Raven League brightened as they remembered how Mr. Pilbeam had paid each of them a shilling apiece.

They weren't smiling when they got down to the docks the next day and actually saw the Oak and Ivy. Unlike the Raven, this pub hadn't seen a mop or a cleaning rag in years. And the owner offered only a shilling—to split among them.

For two hours, Wiggins, Jennie, Owens, and Dooley scrubbed and polished. They saw plenty of suspicious-looking characters muttering with one another over pints of beer and tumblers of gin, but they didn't hear anything that might be a clue.

Finishing at the Oak and Ivy, they moved along High Street to Broad Street and the Midnight Flit. The place was even filthier than the first pub, and this time the owner offered them only sixpence to do the job—half as much as they'd made just before.

The job took longer too. Partly, that was because they had to deal with caked-on dirt. Also, the members of the Raven League were getting tired.

After the owner paid them, they walked slowly down the street in the mid-afternoon sun. Jennie blew a wisp of hair off her sweaty face. "Tell me, please, that you heard something—*anything*—useful."

Wiggins and the others shook their heads. The drinkers at the Midnight Flit were a rough lot. Wiggins could easily imagine any of them slitting a throat. But they turned out to be remarkably close-mouthed. During Wiggins's time with the Baker Street Irregulars, he'd noticed that most criminals grew loud and boastful after a few drinks.

"Maybe smugglers are just naturally more cautious," he muttered as they walked along to Gun Lane and the Bucket.

This place was the seediest and filthiest yet. The owner had only one eye and a scarred pit where the other one had been. From the look of his matted hair—and the smell that came from his clothes—he hadn't bathed in the last year.

He scowled as he listened to the Raven Leaguers' offer of work. "I can't go throwing away no money for cleaning." He paused for a moment. "Tell you what—do the job, and I'll give you a meal."

Wiggins didn't even want to think of what he was scrubbing off the floor. He noticed, however, that none of the benches and tables matched, and much of the furniture had nicks and traces of repairs. *Plenty of barroom brawls in here,* he thought. If the drinkers at this pub were more boisterous, maybe they'd also turn out to be more talkative.

But by the time Wiggins and his friends had finished, the patrons—as scurvy a bunch as Wiggins had ever seen—hadn't said a thing worth spying for.

The ordeal wasn't over, though. Wiggins, Owens, Jennie, and Dooley faced a truly horrible meal. The pub owner's wife did the cooking. She was a fat, blowsy woman who was, if possible, even filthier than her husband. The potatoes were burned; the meat was tasteless, gray, and tough as shoe leather. The plates were greasy and spotted with earlier meals.

Wiggins gritted his teeth and choked the stuff down. This was their payment, after all, and refusing it might make the owner and his patrons suspicious. Pretending to cough, Wiggins spat a piece of gristle into his hand and let it drop to the floor.

The place would be filthy again soon enough. Why should he care?

He was doggedly chewing away when a group of men came swaying and staggering into the Bucket. Wiggins glanced over. *Sailors, by the look of them,* he thought.

After buying a round of drinks, one of the men raised his glass, saying in a slurred voice, "Here's to our friends on the good ship *Sea Foam*, leaving on the tide."

Another of the men brought up his glass as well. "So long as the old tub don't sink on the way to Hamburg."

That brought a roar of drunken laughter from the group. The sailors continued to exchange rude jokes and banter as they slurped gin from their tumblers.

"So," one man said, "are you going to have any passengers without tickets on this trip?"

One of the *Sea Foam's* crewmen nearly spilled his drink from laughing so hard. "Our cap'n has started to discourage regular folk from sailing with us. The old skinflint makes more money from the other kind of cargo. Knowing him, I wouldn't be surprised if he were fiddling the accounts for supplies as well."

"Me, I feel sorry for Mr. Quick," another seaman said. "He has such a hard time keeping workmen at his warehouse."

Wiggins put down his plate. "We can go now."

He got sidelong glances from his friends, but they were happy enough to put down the muck they had been eating. No one said anything until they were well away from the pub. At last, Jennie burst out, "We all heard it, but I'll be hanged if I understand what that sailor said."

"I wouldn't suppose you would," Wiggins replied, "nor Owens, or even Dooley. He's often down around the docks, but he's never been on the river as much as I have."

From the time he started organizing the Baker Street Irregulars, Wiggins had gone out of his way to make friends with people who might help him on jobs for Sherlock Holmes. Some of the most useful had been the river men who ran small boats up, down, and across the river. They'd often given Wiggins rides along the banks of the Thames.

When Dooley's brother had been killed, the boatmen had searched the river and found him.

Wiggins explained this as he led his friends down the street. "Downriver, toward Gravesend, we'd pass a run-down warehouse. In better days, the owner had painted his name on the wall facing the river in letters at least ten feet tall. It's a sort of landmark for the river men. I've seen it a dozen times. And now that I know my letters . . ."

Stepping over to a grimy doorway, he traced five letters on the dirty wood: Q-U-I-C-K.

"Dooley, are any of your dad's mates around here? We need to know when the tide goes out."

"Right over there." Dooley pointed to a knot of men by a wharf. The Raven Leaguers rushed over but let Dooley do the talking.

"That will be this evening, about a quarter after eight," a man with a pockmarked but genial face told them.

Thanking him, they moved off so they wouldn't be overheard. "I think I know how the smugglers work," Wiggins said. "The 'passengers without tickets' wait at the old Quick warehouse. The smugglers come out by boat to deliver their cargo—"

"Human cargo," Jennie muttered.

Owens spoke more plainly. "Crooks on the run."

"—to outgoing ships," Wiggins finished. He glanced up at the sun, trying to judge the time. "That means we have a few hours before the *Sea Foam* sails. So the question is, how can the four of us, and a hunted Indian, scuttle this whole scheme?"

Chapter 14

"IF ONLY MR. HOLMES WERE HERE." DOOLEY'S MOROSE voice seemed to sum up their problem.

"Well, he's not," Wiggins replied. "He's in Scotland, so we can't talk to him. And the police are busy looking for Silent Eagle, so they won't leap onto a suggestion from us to raid the Quick warehouse—"

His eyes grew wide. "Or would they?"

"You usually say the police wouldn't do anything on our say-so," Jennie reminded him.

Wiggins nodded. "But they might go to the warehouse—if they believed Silent Eagle was there."

Jennie looked ready to argue but only stood with her mouth open.

"That's brilliant!" Owens exclaimed. He broke off as a detachment of police officers came marching down the street. They entered each building while scouring every possible outdoor hiding place.

One of the men in blue mopped his red, sweating face. "How long do we have to keep this up?" he asked.

"Inspector Desmond says until we catch the savage," the answer came from a police sergeant. "He's got the lads out all over the East End."

The members of the Raven League hurried away.

"We've got to get Silent Eagle out of Mr. Shears's shop—and the East End," said Wiggins.

"And fast," Owens added.

"How?" Jennie asked. "Silent Eagle stands out in a crowd."

Wiggins's brow furrowed as he thought hard. "Benny Flagg isn't out with his cab. His horse is still recovering—and *he's* still recovering from all the drinks he got after the horse came back. Suppose we rented the cab—"

"Colonel Cody didn't give you enough money to do that," Jennie objected. "And even if you did get it, then you'd have a cab without a horse and driver."

"But we know someone who can solve all those problems, don't we?" Wiggins replied. "Colonel Cody could provide the money and the horse. He could even drive the cab to pick up Silent Eagle—"

"He *could*," Jennie said doubtfully. "But *would* he?"

"Buffalo Bill said he'd do anything to help Silent Eagle," Wiggins said. "We can only ask him. That means a trip to Piccadilly."

"And he can think up a place to stash Silent Eagle too!" Dooley said.

Jim the valet wasn't much pleased to see them, but he took a message to Colonel Cody. A moment later, he was ushering them into Cody's rooms.

"You have news for me?" Buffalo Bill asked eagerly.

Wiggins waited until the servant left, then reported what the members of the Raven League had found out, along with the plan he'd hatched.

Cody nodded and grinned like a young lad. "Deal me in."

"Er—" Jennie looked slightly embarrassed as she spoke up. "I think you'll need a disguise, sir. Your face is on posters all over London."

"By golly, you're right." Buffalo Bill went to the door. "Oh, Jim. Can I borrow that new round hat I saw you wearing?"

The valet stared. "My derby, sir?"

"Yes, I'll need it for this afternoon. On the bright side, though, you've got the rest of the day off."

Jim walked off, muttering about eccentric Americans. Wiggins told Cody how to find the stable where Benny Flagg kept his cab. "We'll take care of a disguise for Silent Eagle," he promised. "Meet us there in an hour and a half—and bring money."

The next hour passed in a blur. The Raven League returned to the East End. Jennie and Dooley went off with more expense money to buy new clothes for Silent Eagle. Now he'd have to look like someone who could afford to ride in a hansom cab. Owens went to Mr. Shears, bringing the news of the coming move. Wiggins began hunting through neighborhood pubs in search of Benny Flagg.

He caught up with the cabman in the Raven, where Benny was working his way through a pint of beer.

"Got some business for you, Benny," Wiggins said.

"I got no business," Flagg responded with a shrug and a beery sigh. "My horse is laid up, and so is my cab."

Wiggins lowered his voice. "I've got a gent who wants to rent your cab."

Benny put down his beer. "Why would someone want to do that?"

"It's for a joke," Wiggins said with a shrug.

"Oh." Benny often told tales of gentlemen who'd had too much to drink and the lengths they went to play pranks and jokes. "Has he got money, then?"

"Come to the stables and see," Wiggins told him.

Flagg almost called off the deal when he saw the apparition awaiting them. Buffalo Bill leaned against a wall well down the line of horse stalls, far away from the open double doors and the light that came in. He had tucked his trademark long auburn hair into the derby. A stained long cloth coat, a duster, covered most of his clothes. He'd turned up the collar of the coat and wound a scarf around as well to hide his face and the distinctive imperial beard and mustache he wore.

Benny began backing away. "I don't think—"

Buffalo Bill reached into his right coat pocket, then opened his hand to reveal a small stack of gleaming coins.

"Five guineas!" Benny gasped. He stared as if mesmerized as Cody brought out his left hand and slowly clinked another five gold coins onto the pile.

"Well," Benny said, licking his lips, "I suppose I can enjoy a joke as well as the next bloke." He rushed down the central aisle of the stables to snatch the offered coins, muttering, "You done me a good turn, young Wiggins. I'll remember that."

Moments later, Benny was scuttling off, his pockets a-jingle, as the stable man showed Buffalo Bill the available horses. Cody broke all the rules of horse-trading, paying heavily for the healthiest-looking cab horse without bargaining. Climbing onto the two-wheeled rig, he leaned over and whispered to Wiggins, "You know, son, as soon as that cabbie gets a few drinks in him, this story will be all over town. We need this business finished, and quick."

Climbing into the passenger's compartment in the front of the cab, Wiggins sat as Cody whipped up the cab horse, taking them out of the stables. Minutes later, following Wiggins's directions, they pulled up in front of Mr. Shears's barbershop. Wiggins spotted Jennie and Dooley peering out between the multiple panes of glass.

As Wiggins leaped to the pavement, the shop door opened and Owens led out an elderly invalid. Wiggins blinked. *Wait a tick! That's Silent Eagle!*

The Indian walked slowly, with a slight crouch. He had a white shirt and a tie under a slightly worn but still presentable jacket. Over his shoulders he wore a shawl, using it to shade his features. After taking a careful look, Wiggins had to grin. Apparently, Mr. Shears had added an artistic touch, powdering Silent Eagle's face to give him some pallor.

When he climbed into the cab and sat back, the Sioux warrior looked like any other London cab passenger. Cody gave the Raven Leaguers an appreciative nod and started the cab off at a sedate pace for his rooms in Piccadilly.

Wiggins rubbed his hands together. "Now all we have to do is find Inspector Des—"

As if on cue, Inspector Desmond came around the corner, heading toward them. "We've had several reports of people spotting your Indian friend hereabouts," he said with a smile. "So we're starting a house-to-house search."

Wiggins sent up a silent prayer of thanks that they'd just sent Silent Eagle on his way. "Actually, we were looking for you, sir," he said. "We think Silent Eagle is hiding farther along the river, in a warehouse."

Desmond frowned as Wiggins spun a quick story about spotting the Indian skulking around the old Quick warehouse. Then Desmond nodded. "Right. We'd better get over there and have a look, shouldn't we?"

He gazed down the street, and Wiggins's heart sank. Buffalo Bill's cab had gotten caught behind an unloading wagon. "I say! Cab! Cab!" Desmond called after it. He began moving toward the disguised Western hero, with the members of the Raven League trailing nervously behind.

"Oh!" the policeman said as he got closer to the cab. "It's taken." He shrugged and looked back at Wiggins and the others. "Well, a hansom would have been a tight fit for all of us. Let's go round here and see if we can't hail a growler."

That was a narrow squeak, Wiggins thought, his heart returning to its normal pace.

Soon, they were boarding a larger, four-wheeled cab. Wiggins boosted Dooley into the seat beside Desmond while he, Jennie, and Owens sat facing the inspector.

As they rattled along the streets to the riverside, Wiggins glanced at his friends. They looked as nervous as he felt. This was not falling out the way he'd imagined. He'd expected Desmond to gather up as many constables as he could and then rush off to surround the warehouse. Instead, the inspector apparently intended to scout the area first and wanted them along.

Desmond dismissed their cab some distance from the warehouse, then slowly approached the building on foot. "The place certainly looks deserted," he said to Wiggins. "Are you sure this is where you saw him?"

"This is where we saw him," Wiggins insisted.

"Aren't you going to get some reinforcements?" Jennie asked in a worried voice.

"I think we'll take a look first." The police inspector walked right up to the door and pushed it open.

Wiggins's jaw dropped. He couldn't believe this copper was going in alone! Did Desmond have some clever plan up his sleeve?

Desmond peered inside, then stepped in. "Doesn't seem to be anyone here, but it is fairly dark—"

The copper was just strolling into a smugglers' den! Wiggins darted forward, followed by his friends. Even though his eyes weren't used to the dimness inside, he spotted several people in the large, echoing room. *Desmond must have been dazzled by the sunlight not to see them,* he thought.

Five of the figures retreated into the deeper shadows. Two came forward. Wiggins saw familiar faces—Zeke Black and Chinless Ed Gorham. He pointed at the American gangster. "That man is a wanted fugitive from the United States." Wiggins glanced over his shoulder, sincerely hoping that Inspector Desmond had brought a gun.

Instead, he saw that Desmond had retreated to the warehouse door—and was closing it. "So, you found out about that too," the inspector said. "It seems you've discovered all our little secrets, except one. I work with these people." His voice grew harder. "Or, more precisely, *they* work for *me*."

Zeke Black closed in on the Raven Leaguers, his initial look of surprise turning into a scowl. Beside him, Chinless Ed Gorham held up a small pocket pistol.

Wiggins and his dismayed friends turned to face Inspector Desmond. He leaned back, arms crossed, blocking the door that led back to sunlight and safety.

"Oh, I'm not the chief of this operation," the rogue policeman said mildly. "There are others whom I work for. They told me how you and Mr. Holmes had already involved yourselves in their business."

"You—" Jennie choked on her words. "You're a police officer. But you work for people who have plotted against the *law*?"

"Against the Crown," Desmond corrected her. "We have a shared interest in keeping things as they were meant to be, keeping people in their proper places—unlike our American cousins, with their foolish democratic notions."

Owens's eyes narrowed. "And the proper place for most folks is *down*?"

"Good lad. You know what I mean, right enough." Desmond's lips twisted beneath his immaculately trimmed mustache. "People over here are picking up ridiculous American ideas. The last thing we need is our nations coming closer. That's what a popular American like this Cody creature could achieve."

"So you went out to get him and his Indians in trouble?" Dooley asked.

"Cody's sudden celebrity caught our leaders by surprise," Desmond admitted. "They wanted to dampen the public's admiration for Cody, and that meddling constable gave us the perfect opportunity. After we dealt with him, our political connections worked to exploit the situation."

Desmond sneered. "They often used that idiot Pryke to stir up the rabble. A small investment to rent the beginnings of a mob, and he certainly set the lower classes afire. The man overreached himself, however, shooting his mouth off about people who were not to be mentioned. His punishment helped fan the anti-American flames to a gratifying height, though."

"You mean after Pryke mentioned the 'higher-ups' that day we saw you," Wiggins asked, "you had his head broken?"

He suddenly felt angry with himself. *I should have seen this,* he thought. *When we first approached him, Desmond told us he'd already heard that the gun had gone missing from Buffalo Bill's Wild West. But Nate Salsbury, who knows everything that goes on at the show, said he hadn't mentioned it. So where did Desmond find that out?*

Now Wiggins realized that the information could only have come from Constable Turnbuckle's attackers.

"You four have shown unexpected ingenuity," Desmond said, "although it put you in the middle of another of our ventures. At first we gave all the credit to Sherlock Holmes."

Dooley suddenly stepped forward, his face a pale mask. Obviously, he'd been putting Desmond's hints together. "These people you work for—*they* had my brother killed to keep their secrets. I felt better because the man who did it got caught, but he died in his cell. Was that because of your precious bosses too?"

"You mean Bruiser Rowley?" Desmond gave Dooley a cold smile. "He knew too much. And that murder charge might have pried some information out of him if he weren't silenced. You should thank me, boy. I *personally* dealt with your brother's murderer."

Dooley looked as if he were going to be sick. Desmond didn't even appear to notice. "My expectations were for more of an executive role in the organization. Instead, I found myself involved in a duel of wits with a bunch of children."

His handsome face took on a hard and cruel expression. "That charade I staged by the docks should have scared you off, or at least persuaded you to give me the information I wanted."

His eyes narrowed. "Now is the time to reconsider your situation. I assure you, young Wiggins, mine is the winning side. We've used this operation to bring in a number of useful agents unknown in this country." He nodded toward Chinless Ed, standing guard beside Zeke Black. Then he turned his gaze to the group of men hiding in the shadows. "We've also moved many 'clients' out of Britain, creating a web of people who will do our bidding all over Europe."

"You dress like a posh bloke and talk about 'we,'" Wiggins shot back, "but to the real posh blokes, there's not much difference between you and Pryke and me. They're using you to get what they want so they don't have to dirty their own hands."

Black and Gorham tensed, ready to punish Wiggins for his bold words. But Desmond stopped them with a dismissive wave of his hand. "You flatter yourself for the small part you played in thwarting my superiors' last little effort."

Wiggins's eyes grew wide. "You were part of that?" he asked.

Desmond grinned. "I played a small part too," he admitted. "But I'm to take a larger hand in our next project. When all is ready, we'll unleash a stroke that will bring this city to its knees."

Chapter 15

INSPECTOR DESMOND FLICKED THE END OF HIS NEATLY trimmed mustache. "By the end of our campaign, we will be masters of the British Empire. You have a chance to establish a position for yourselves, depending on how forthcoming you are in the course of our next chat." The rogue policeman turned to Zeke Black. "You and Gorham make sure our visitors are properly secured."

Desmond started walking away, then glanced over his shoulder. "And Black—no mistakes this time, eh?"

The roustabout's surly face went red with anger, but he said nothing until Desmond had moved out of earshot. Then he turned to Chinless Ed Gorham. "Keep the gun on them, you. *I'll* tie them up."

The American's face went as red as his companion's. "Now, wait a minute, Zeke. I can tie knots." Gorham had a flat, nasal accent when he spoke, along with a whining tone in his voice. With his receding chin and ridiculous mustache, he would have seemed comical, except for the look in his eyes—and the pistol in his hand.

"I put in two years on a riverboat," Zeke Black replied. "I know the ropes." He didn't bother to hide the contempt in his voice. "And Desmond just told me to get the job done right."

"Aw, Zeke, don't start with that again," Gorham complained, his voice getting whinier.

"You worked on a riverboat?" Even getting tied up couldn't dampen Dooley's curiosity. "In the Wild West?"

"Nah," Black replied, "on the Saskatchewan River in Canada. That's where I come from. Knocked about quite a bit out West, both north and south of the border."

"All of it honest work, no doubt," Wiggins said sarcastically.

That actually got a laugh from Black. "Maybe not. But it all made plenty of money for me. I was good enough in my line of work that—certain people—approached me to get involved in what they called 'a profitable enterprise.' All I had to do was get a position with the Wild West show."

He smirked. "It was easy enough getting around that fathead Cody. Although his partner was harder to buffalo—Salsbury is nobody's fool."

"Goody for you." Jennie spoke up. "Too bad you and your friend weren't as good with a real buffalo."

Her comment made Chinless Ed twitch. "Say, I paid a bundle to get out of New York. Figured I'd be sailing in style, not hiding out as the tender to that monster. Zeke got him on the wagon, but I didn't know what to do when he handed me that rope. It wasn't my fault—"

"It was *all* your fault!" Zeke Black barked, jerking on the ropes as he tied Wiggins's wrists. Wiggins winced in pain. Any chance of wriggling out of those bonds had just gone out the window.

The Canadian outlaw glared at the New York gangster. "You spooked the stupid beast when we got to Earl's Court, making that copper notice you. Then, when I told you to lie low while we got the

buffalo into the corral, you go and steal a gun—
Buffalo Bill's gun, no less."

"I carried an equalizer every day of my life since I was ten years old," Gorham replied. "It's like I was naked without one. So when I saw the Colt sitting out there in the middle of that fancy tent—" He broke off at the look Black gave him. Then, pulling himself together, he began waving around the gun in his hand. "Besides, it came in handy enough when that cop came after us. Not that I'da knowed he was a cop in regular clothes."

"What happened?" Owens asked.

"He showed a badge as we left the show grounds, by the stable bridge." Black shook his head as he tied up Owens. "Just when I would have passed Chinless Ed along the chain and been rid of him."

"Well, what kind of luck was it that the guy would recognize me from a cartoon in a magazine?" Chinless Ed protested.

"Bad luck!" Zeke burst out. "That's the only kind of luck you brought with you from America."

"And then the stupid gun turned out not to have real bullets in it," Gorham went on. "I laid the guy out with the butt end. Should have finished him when he was down."

"It's not every day a copper gets shot in London," Black responded, "even with blank bullets. If we'd killed him as well, the police would be tearing the city apart looking for us. Better to leave him as we did, in no shape to talk and with the law looking for some savage."

"*You're* the savages," Dooley cried as Zeke moved past him. "Silent Eagle saved lives that day. But you people take 'em—coppers', kids', even my brother's!"

Dooley spat in Black's face. The angry cowboy laid him flat with a backhand slap. Jennie let out a shriek and jumped on him. Zeke easily flung her back and raised his hand to strike her as well. Wiggins and Owens tried to kick out at him till Gorham pressed his gun barrel to Wiggins's temple.

"Won't bother me one bit to do you in right now," the American growled. "And this gun's got real bullets. So don't move, either of you."

Zeke quickly grabbed Jennie and tied her hands. "Soon enough, we'll find the Indian and do for him." He gave the ropes an extra-vicious tug. "After all the noise in the newspapers passes, we'll take care of Turnbuckle so it looks as if he died in his sleep at the hospital. Then everything can go back to business as usual."

Wiggins's insides went cold. If that was the plan, things didn't look good for the Raven League. They'd be the only ones who knew about the smuggling ring besides the people running it. These ruthless men weren't likely to let Wiggins and his friends live to tell the tale.

Black didn't realize what he'd given away. He was busy giving Gorham dark looks. "So far, the police have been looking in the wrong places because of that little trick I learned from the Indians up in Saskatchewan."

Dooley stared. "*You* scalped the copper?"

"It sure wasn't him." Black jerked his head in Gorham's direction. "Between that and leaving Cody's gun beside the copper, it should have been enough to keep everyone's eyes on the Americans."

He scowled. "While I was doing the job, I asked Chinless over there to do one little thing. 'Get rid of that magazine,' I said. He could have burned it or taken it away to dump in the Thames or chuck on a trash pile. What does he do? He tosses it onto the railway embankment to be found by you. All my hard work comes to nothing, and Desmond cuts up nasty about *me* making mistakes."

Gorham was busy waving his revolver again. "Don't call me Chinless!"

One of the criminals waiting to be smuggled out of the country came over. He was handsome in a skinny, foppish sort of way. Blond hair tumbled into his blue eyes as he stood by Gorham. Wiggins recognized him, having seen him around various thieves' dens in the East End—Gentleman Jeremy Clive, the jewel thief who'd killed someone during his last burglary.

"I say, old boy," Gentleman Jeremy said in his posh voice, "from a business viewpoint, these witnesses are deuced inconvenient. Better to do away with them now and leave them to the Thames after we go—"

"If they're that inconvenient, why don't you do it yourself?" Inspector Desmond reappeared, leering at Gentleman Jeremy, who drew back.

Desmond shook his head. "Rather leave it to the servants, would you? Actually *doing* the job might distress your gentlemanly sensibilities?"

Clive retreated to the other skulking fugitives as if Desmond had whipped him.

Zeke Black hustled the members of the Raven League into a line as Desmond turned back. "Neatly done," the inspector told him. "Gag them as well."

"I thought you wanted us to talk," Wiggins said.

"Oh, I do indeed," Desmond replied. "I'm reasonably sure you know where Silent Eagle is hiding—probably because you put him there. But everything in its place, and this isn't the place where I'll be asking you. I've just exchanged messages with the higher-ups. We'll move our chat to another house, a bit quieter. No traffic on the river or streets outside."

Wiggins couldn't keep the fear from his eyes as Black gagged him. Desmond noticed, leaning forward to say, "This is just to make sure there's no foolishness on the journey. I'm sure you'll see reason without the need for any . . . extreme measures."

Desmond smiled. "See here, Wiggins. You can't tell me you've suddenly become fond of this heathen. Heaven knows what he's done—who he's killed—back in America. He could have dozens of hanging offenses in his past. Let us have him. Afterward, we'll set you all free. On the off chance anyone listens to you, we'll change our operations a bit. Gorham will go off to Hamburg on the *Sea Foam*, and that will be an end to it."

This bloke should have been an actor, Wiggins thought. *Even though I know what will really happen, that he's lying through his teeth, part of me wants to believe him.*

"Just think about that during the ride." Desmond ordered Black to hitch up a pair of horses to a wagon. The inspector and Gorham unlatched the tailgate and carried the members of the Raven League, one by one, to deposit them in the wagon bed. While Black harnessed the horses, Desmond and Gorham covered the prisoners with a canvas tarpaulin.

Lying in the darkness, Wiggins heard Desmond say, "Looks as if we're ready to go. Black, you drive. Gorham, open the doors." He raised his voice. "And Clive, you can close them, if you don't mind. Gorham will be joining us."

The wagon lurched into motion. Wiggins was already moving, twisting his arms and hips, trying to get one of his bound hands into the right pocket of his trousers. For once his oversize clothes were an advantage. By yanking on the waistband of the trousers, he managed to bring the pocket a little closer.

Wiggins fumbled inside his pocket. The tight ropes cut the circulation to his hand, making it clumsy. But he finally managed to get hold of the penknife he always carried. He'd found it in a back alley, where it had probably been tossed away as trash. Half the bone inlay on the handle had cracked away, and the larger blade had snapped off.

But there was still the smaller blade, which Wiggins unfolded by feel. It seemed awfully small compared to the ropes it would have to cut. The wagon rattled over the brick floor of the warehouse, then onto the cobblestones outside. Sunlight seeping through the tightly woven canvas lightened things slightly for the captives. Wiggins brought the knife around and began sawing at his bonds.

It seemed to take forever as they clattered along, but at last, the rope holding his wrists together parted. Stretching out his freed hand, Wiggins poked Owens and passed the knife over to him.

Worming his way across the wooden floor of the wagon, he headed for the edge of the tarpaulin. Wiggins worked the gag off his face and stuck his head out. For a moment, he blinked in the sunlight, then breathed a stifled sigh of relief. The three men on the driver's seat were all facing forward. They hadn't noticed that he'd gotten free.

Not that there was anything much Wiggins could do. Not with his friends still bound and helpless.

Wiggins raised his head a little higher to see over the tail of the wagon. They were moving along a narrow street right by the Thames. Other wagons and carts moved around them. Behind them, Wiggins spotted a hansom cab.

His eyes went big as he recognized the derby on the cab's driver. And the muffled-up passenger was now throwing constricting clothing away as the cab picked up speed.

Instead of leaving the East End for Piccadilly, Cody must have decided to follow Desmond and the Raven Leaguers. Then he had trailed the wagon when he saw Desmond, Black, and Gorham leaving the warehouse.

Now he'd obviously spotted Wiggins because Buffalo Bill and Silent Eagle weren't just following—they were racing in pursuit!

Chapter 16

WIGGINS LAY FROZEN AND UNNOTICED HALFWAY under the tarpaulin, his eyes darting back and forth from the hansom cab behind to the driver's seat up in front of the wagon. Perhaps the accelerated clatter of the hansom's wheels against the cobblestones caught Zeke Black's ears. Maybe it was the shouted complaints from the other carters at the cab's sudden burst of speed. Whatever the reason, the Canadian outlaw glanced back just as the cab hit a gap in the pavement. The concealing derby flew off, and Buffalo Bill's hair streamed out in the breeze behind him.

Zeke looked thunderstruck as he recognized who was quickly coming up behind them. He snapped the reins, speeding up his own team, and shouted something to his companions.

Chinless Ed Gorham stood up to take a wobbly stance between Zeke and Inspector Desmond, fumbling in his coat pocket. He pulled out his little revolver and turned to aim at the pursuers, who by now had drawn alongside.

As soon as Wiggins saw the pistol, he hurled himself at Gorham's gun hand, pushing upward so the shot missed. Gorham flung him back, tumbling Wiggins on top of his companions under the tarp.

Wiggins found himself staring down the gun barrel as Chinless Ed took furious aim at him. But before Gorham could fire, Buffalo Bill cracked his whip right in the gangster's face. Gorham staggered back, his flailing arms sending Inspector Desmond's hat flying. The gun in his hand went off twice into the air, and Chinless Ed toppled over onto Zeke Black.

In a tangle of arms and legs, the two men nearly fell to the roadway. Zeke lost the reins, and the wagon suddenly shot forward as the horses took off.

Furious shouts came from the drivers struggling to pull their vehicles out of the way as the wagon raced onward, weaving wildly along the quay-side road. Wiggins was ready to add some cries of his own—of sheer terror. But Black and Desmond hadn't seen him yet, so Wiggins kept low, waiting till his friends got free. From the bumping and fluttering of the tarpaulin, Jennie, Owens, and Dooley had to be well on the way.

Buffalo Bill urged his cab horse forward, trying to catch up again. Inspector Desmond was bent over on the driver's seat, scrabbling for something on the floorboards—the revolver, Wiggins suddenly realized.

Cody's cab almost pulled up beside them again, but the runaway wagon careened against it with a shock. As Gorham and Desmond struggled to hold on to the wagon, Zeke Black cannoned from the driver's seat. He landed in the river with a tremendous splash.

Chinless Ed let out a yelp as he nearly tumbled after Zeke. Desmond hauled him back by the tail of his coat. The out-of-control wagon lurched back and forth across the narrow road, going far too fast. If they didn't crash into another wagon or cart, they'd end up smashing into the low retaining wall.

Wiggins tried not to think of the terrifying possibilities—breaking their necks, dashing their brains out on the pavement, or being flung into the Thames to drown. Whatever the choice, things didn't look good for him or his friends.

Buffalo Bill zigzagged after them, bringing his cab up on the left-hand side of the wagon, trying to keep between them and the wall. The hansom cab's wheels clashed against the side of the wagon, causing both vehicles to shudder. Wiggins clamped his hands to the wooden side of the wagon, fearful he'd catapult over.

Up on the driver's seat of the wagon, Chinless Ed Gorham blundered to his feet, panic written all over his face. He'd managed to recover his pistol, waving it wildly in one hand as he clung to the seat with the other. The horses pulling the wagon swerved again, and Gorham lost his hold. With a high-pitched scream, he fell off and landed on the cobblestones below. His screaming ended abruptly.

Wiggins swallowed heavily.

In the sudden silence, he heard Owens's annoyed voice. "Hold still, will you? I've nearly got you loose."

A second later, Jennie wriggled out from under the tarpaulin. At first she squinted in the sunlight. Then her eyes went wide with horror as she realized what was going on.

"Hold tight," Wiggins advised her as Buffalo Bill brought his hansom cab up level with them again. This time, Silent Eagle stood crouched on the seat of the open cab. He'd thrown away most of the disguise the Raven Leaguers had assembled for him, keeping only his shirt and trousers.

Wiggins was amazed at the way the Indian maintained his balance, seeming almost to foresee any bounces or bumps. Dooley and Owens popped out from under the tarpaulin just as a missing paving stone sent the cab into a major bound, and Silent Eagle took that moment to jump.

The Indian literally flew over the crouched children to land right behind the driver's seat. At the noise, Inspector Desmond whirled from trying to recapture the reins. He had fallen far from his usual elegant self. His hair was mussed, his face flushed, his features twisted in a wordless snarl. He flung himself at Silent Eagle, trying to send the Indian over the side to suffer the same fate that had taken Chinless Ed.

Silent Eagle grappled with his antagonist in a fierce hand-to-hand struggle. Neither man was armed, but Silent Eagle was simply trying to subdue Desmond, while the renegade policeman fought with murder in his heart. Desmond reared back and head-butted Silent Eagle in the face. Yet even with blood streaming from his nose and mouth, the Indian held on.

The inspector began thrashing violently, not trying to attack, but to get free of Silent Eagle's grip. Desmond succeeded as their vehicle swerved away from the river and toward a heavy dray wagon. Desmond jumped, aiming for the bales of cotton in the wagon bed.

Wiggins never saw him land. The terrified team of horses swung over again, flinging Wiggins flat. He pushed himself upright and froze.

Up ahead, the river went into a bend, and so did the road. At the speed the horses were going, the wagon would never make that curve. Gulping, Wiggins realized they'd have to jump!

But when he turned, he found Jennie clambering onto the driver's seat. Somehow, she'd gotten hold of the reins for the left-hand horse in the team.

Wiggins made his way to the other side of the wagon and looked over. His heart sank as he saw the only means of controlling the other animal trailing along on the ground.

Silent Eagle helped Jennie get into position and brace herself. They spoke for a moment, heads close. Jennie nodded.

Then Silent Eagle turned and launched himself onto the back of the right-hand horse.

The astonished animal almost stumbled, which would have sent them spinning into a crash. But somehow, Silent Eagle managed to stay balanced and steady his mount, getting hold of the lost reins. With the Indian controlling one horse and Jennie hauling on the reins of the other, they managed to slow the headlong rush. The horses were tired, their sides covered with lathery sweat. They slowed, taking the wagon safely around the curve in the road, and finally stopped.

Immediately, a crowd gathered around them. Several carters ran up to grab the bridles on the horses, making sure they went nowhere. Not that Wiggins thought that was likely. The animals stood on trembling legs, their heads low, blowing great breaths of air.

"What happened to Chinless Ed and the others?" Dooley demanded.

"Better you don't know," Wiggins replied, his voice almost lost among the exclamations from the crowd.

"Wotcher think ye're doing, then?"

"That was a neat bit of driving, the two of you."

"Have to be mad to try something like that."

From his vantage point above the hubbub, Wiggins saw Buffalo Bill rein in the hansom cab, jump down from his perch, and head for the wagon. Wiggins also spotted several figures in blue making their way toward them.

"All right, then, what's this all about?" The lead constable was a grizzled veteran with sergeant's stripes.

Buffalo Bill stepped up to him. "My friend and I were chasing a bunch of bad characters who'd kidnapped these children."

The sergeant's eyes narrowed at the accent and at Buffalo Bill's long hair. "American are you, then?"

"Colonel William F. Cody," the Westerner introduced himself. "And my friend is Silent Eagle, whom I'm sure you've heard about."

At the mention of Silent Eagle's name, several of the constables began closing in. Buffalo Bill held up a hand. "Constable Turnbuckle's real attacker got himself run over during the chase," he said, "but not before he let off a couple of shots. More important, the young folks on the wagon were kidnapped because they discovered a smuggling ring. A sort of Underground Railway for criminals."

"There's a lot of them hiding out not too far away," Wiggins chimed in. "They're waiting for a ship at the old Quick warehouse."

The sergeant frowned, thinking over this news.

Buffalo Bill stepped beside Silent Eagle as the Indian came down off the horse he'd been riding. "The two of us are at your disposal. But I strongly hope you'll take a moment to check the warehouse before conducting us wherever we have to go."

Wiggins watched the struggle on the sergeant's face. Here he had a bird in hand. But the sergeant was a veteran, a man who knew his business. Now he showed he could recognize someone who knew his business as well. "We'll take a look right now," he said.

"You may want to telegraph the river police," Wiggins added. "Those ginks are sure to have a boat."

On the route back to the warehouse, the sergeant left one of his men to guard the remains of Chinless Ed Gorham, now covered with a horse blanket.

As for Zeke Black and Inspector Desmond, they found no sign. Black, however, must have returned to Quick's with a warning. The police found the warehouse empty, but from the wharf outside, they saw a four-oar boat shoving off onto the river. The sergeant recognized one of the people aboard—the only one who was rowing efficiently. "Gentleman Jeremy Clive!" he burst out.

The fugitives didn't get very far. A river police steam launch soon appeared. On hearing the sergeant's report about who was aboard, the launch set off in speedy pursuit, intercepting the boat. Trapped on the river, Gentleman Jeremy and his fellow criminals had no choice but to surrender.

Word of Buffalo Bill's involvement in the affair spread quickly. By the time the sergeant and his charges reached the local police station, reporters were already on hand, and very soon, several of Colonel Cody's prominent friends from London society put in an appearance.

"Maybe we wouldn't have had all this mess if they'd shown their faces a bit earlier," Wiggins muttered.

"That's just the way of society people," Jennie replied. "If you're in trouble, they don't want to know you. When you're in the chips, though, you have plenty of friends." She paused for a second. "Come to think of it, that's the way most respectable people act."

"But not all of 'em." Wiggins looked at her with a smile.

The police questioned Buffalo Bill and the members of the Raven League as well as the captured fugitives. An annoyed Gentleman Jeremy apparently talked very freely. Soon, a bulletin was going out for the apprehension of former Inspector Desmond, and Silent Eagle was walking out with Colonel Cody—free and clear.

"I'm sorry, Silent Eagle." Dooley lowered his head as he approached the Indian.

"Why?"

"I—I said bad things," Dooley stammered, "about you and your people—"

"You and your friends said you would help me." The Indian dropped to one knee so his eyes were level with Dooley's. "And you did. Those are the words I will remember." He looked into the eyes of Wiggins, Jennie, and Owens. "Pahaska told me of your Raven tribe. It is a good thing to have so much trust."

He smiled at the children, then up at Buffalo Bill. "It is a thing we should all remember."

Chapter 17

"You young'uns just hold tight, and you'll enjoy your ride on the Deadwood Stage." John Nelson, the stagecoach guard, smiled at them through his grizzled, chest-long beard. "My own little ones have ridden dozens of times—even on the roof." He and his Indian wife had five children. Jennie had seen the younger ones playing among the tents in the Wild West encampment.

She tried not to look too dubious as Nelson slammed the door on the famous Deadwood Stage. Its paint had worn away in many places, and the wood of the bodywork was dinged and gouged. There were wide enough gaps between the boards in the door to put a finger through. Eighteen years ago, this stagecoach had brought passengers along dangerous roads to a famous Western town.

Nowadays, it helped to provide a thrilling moment for Buffalo Bill's Wild West. Jennie wondered whether or not the old relic shouldn't have been retired years ago.

With a snap of the reins, the coach's team leaped forward. The wheels rolled, and ancient springs groaned in protest, making the coach bounce wildly.

The members of the Raven League had received a special invitation to attend this performance. As the guests of honor, they got to participate in the climax.

"Chief Tall-Like-Oak said he would tell the Buffalo Soldiers about me," Owens said as he struggled to stay in his seat. "One of them might send me a patch from his uniform. Maybe I'll even see them one day."

"You know, not too long ago, four kings rode in this coach, with the Prince of Wales up on the driver's seat beside Buffalo Bill," Wiggins said.

"You mean my behind might be bumping where some king was sitting?" Dooley asked.

"Well, if this thing didn't shake apart then, it shouldn't happen now," Jennie quipped. "I daresay we're a lot lighter."

Still, she had to admit, Buffalo Bill's visit might have done more good than he ever expected. She'd read newspaper stories about the British and American governments working to set up an international court that could settle future problems between them fairly and peacefully. If that came about, one reason would certainly be the good feelings caused by Buffalo Bill's Wild West.

The stagecoach rattled into the arena. From one side, Jennie could see the painted backdrop of Western scenery. From the other, she saw the grandstand full of applauding audience members. They passed the royal box, where J. Montague Pryke sat clapping loud and hard. His head was swathed in so many bandages, at first glance he seemed to be wearing a turban.

Pryke had suddenly become a great friend of all things American after a flood of newspaper stories about the dockside rescue. Reporters happily cast Buffalo Bill as the hero, saving a group of kidnapped children and exposing the criminal-smuggling ring. As far as Jennie read, Colonel Cody had done everything but swim out to capture the boat full of fleeing criminals. Constable Turnbuckle recovered enough to tell his story about Zeke Black and Chinless Ed Gorham. Gorham now occupied an unmarked grave in the Tower Hamlets Cemetery. Black had been captured trying to board a ship for Canada, but Inspector Desmond had vanished. Had he made a successful getaway with the help of the shadowy higher-ups? Or had they simply disposed of him as a failed tool?

After the stagecoach circled once around the arena, the Indians made their appearance, streaming in from behind the painted scenery, yelling and firing guns into the air.

Leaning out the window, Jennie looked at the riders, finally picking Silent Eagle out of the pack of pursuers. He had made his face almost unrecognizable with daubs of war paint.

After a few minutes of howling pursuit by the Indians, a throng of cowboys charged into the arena. Led by Buffalo Bill, they thundered to the rescue of the stage and its passengers. A great deal more gunpowder was burnt as cowboys and Indians exchanged volleys, firing off blank cartridges while the show's cowboy band played the stirring song "Garryowen." The crowd roared approval. Catching Jennie's eye, Buffalo Bill doffed his Stetson hat.

But a sudden chilling thought made her grip the window frame harder as she turned to her friends.

"It's easy enough to know you've got an enemy when he paints his face," she said. "But twice now, we've come up against people who do evil, but they do it in secret. We couldn't even tell who the enemy was. He might be a fine gentleman, or an important official in the government"—Jennie took a deep breath—"or a policeman."

Maybe it was the excitement of the moment. Or maybe, Jennie had to admit, it was justifiable pride that made Wiggins puff up his chest as he responded to her worries. "P'raps we blundered into the fight those times," Wiggins admitted. "But we beat 'em anyway. And from now on, we'll be ready for 'em, won't we?"

Owens nodded. "Right!"

"That's the Raven League," Dooley crowed, bouncing in his seat, "ready for anything!"